A Chief Jack Donaldson Story

Chapter 1

I had the whole world in my hand, or so I thought back in 1986. Being a police chief for the small town in Massachusetts called Essex. Essex was so small where I mean I literally knew of everyone in the town, including their children. I had been in the force for ten years as at the time I was fresh out of the air force and there was no formal police training. I was just thrown in with what training I had out of the air force as I started in this job as a way of making ends meet for my family as my wife and I had just had a newborn son before I joined the force. For the better part of that decade, I usually just dealt with speeders and trespassers, but one night was different from all the others that would change things for good.

It was July third, a Friday night shortly after ten, when we got our first call for the night. I had to answer as the operator had gone on a fifteen-minute break.

"Hello, you've reached Chief Jack Donaldson, Essex Police Department. Please state your emergency."

"Hey, Jack, this is Bobby down at Bothways Farm. I want to report a person trespassing. Please hurry!"

Before I could ask if there was anyone hurt, Bobby hung up on me. I grabbed my coffee and drove over to see what the commotion was. When I was driving through town, I kept a lookout for anything suspicious on my way through but saw nothing as I kept going to the call. I pulled up to the farm where Bobby was awaiting me. He was high strung, pacing back and forth.

"You didn't bring any back up?"

"Bobby, who the fuck are you to question my job? No, for fuck's sake, there's usually nothing ever going on to require back up! What the fuck is going on here?"

"I was about to turn in for the night when we heard the door to the barn slam open. I didn't have the nerve to go out to check on it until you arrived."

He looked as though he was losing his patience with me as he was already angered by the situation, and with that as well as the surrounding area being quiet and wooded, I knew this call could be real. I didn't want to alarm Bobby as Bobby had lived out in the middle of nowhere for years and he was already high strung if he heard even a creak in the woods. But as had prepared myself for what I may find I thought of all the anxiety ridden calls he had done over the years and all of them ended with him telling me to go fuck off.

"Ah, that's what I would want, Bobby. It's better you be safe than sorry. Now let's go check out the barn."

I knew the landscape because I had worked as a caretaker for the greenhouse on the farm before I landed on the police force. We strolled down his gravel driveway slowly as we crept up to the barn. At first glance, the door had looked closed but as we got closer, it was clearly partially open. We strolled into the dark-as-fuck barn as slow as when I would hunt for deer. As I shined my flashlight in and around, my handgun right underneath it, we saw the horses stirring a bit. We then crept up on the window that overlooked the cattle and as I peeked out into the moonlit pasture, they all seemed untouched. We finally made it to the sheep, but there was dead silence. I swallowed. When I shined the flashlight down upon where the sheep should've been, it was empty. I looked over at Bobby and he was just as scared in that moment; neither of us would have guessed someone would do such a thing. Suddenly, we heard a truck gate and doors closing. We couldn't get our feet started quick enough to run outside to see what was happening.

"Fuck!!! Jack, these people are getting away!"

We ran outside to see a dark trailer and truck driving away with sounds of scared sheep in the trailer. I threw my gun back in my holster and decided that I'd follow them.

"Bobby, stay behind and watch everything. I'm going to see if I can catch these people."

"Be careful Jack!"

I hopped up in the Bronco, but instead of putting on the lights and the siren, as I hadn't wanted to give my location away, I radioed into the station as I took off. Our dispatch, Tom Wheeler, was back always my person I'd have with me while I was on shift, and he was the best damn dispatcher a department could have. *"Tom, this is Jack. I'm currently leaving Bothways Farm, in pursuit of a truck that is carrying a herd of sheep that were just stolen from the farm."*

"Jack, do you need backup?"

"No, I should be fine. Just in case, why don't you notify Marylin."

Marylin was one of my top deputies on the force; she has been with us for two years now. When I hired her, Tom had thought I had something for her or maybe he did and wanted to cover that up so no one would know. But she was a damn good deputy and a right-hand person I always went to in tough situations.

"Ok, over and out. I'll be here if you need any backup."

I was born and raised here, so I knew all the roads that covered the town. It would serve as an advantage in a situation that had never occurred for me in my tenure on the force until now as I made my way through all the side streets to finally reach the causeway. I was driving down the causeway over the river when up ahead I saw the truck getting ready to pass the last restaurant at the end. I sped it up a bit, knowing if they made it beyond the causeway that I'd have trouble catching them as it was more densely populated heading into the next town. A quarter of the way to them, they turned left heading towards the station. I ramped the speed up a bit until I turned and was right upon them. I quickly turned my lights on to pull them over. They stopped directly across from the police station and as I came to a stop myself, I radioed in, *"Tommy, can you run Wyoming plate 395 TW8?"*

I was patiently awaiting Tom's response when the driver's door popped open, and my heart loudly thudded up in my throat. "GET BACK IN YOUR VEHICLE, NOW!" I screamed. Thankfully, the guy listened, and Tom came back with his response.

"Uh, Jack, it's registered to a Frank Munroe."

"Is that who I think it is Tommy?"

"If you are referring to the slandered sheep farmer from the Midwest then yes. He's got lawsuits pending against him for the theft of livestock. I'm sending Marylin over to assist, what's your position?"

"Right across the street."

"Wait, really? Oh, hello there buddy. Copy."

I took a deep breath at that moment before I slowly opened the door and got out of the Bronco. As I came up on the trailer, the sheep were yapping at me. I had drawn my flashlight so I could see who was in the truck, and sure enough, it was Frank. *What the hell is he doing here? Why would he be doing something that he's been accused of let alone denied?* I was about to find out.

I tapped on the window, and as he rolled it down, there was a huge man in the passenger seat, and I mean muscular huge. If there was anything going down here, I knew I would need backup soon.

"Hello, officer, what tends to be the issue tonight?"

"Well first, don't act coy with me. Second, you should know why I'm pulling you over right now!"

"Do you know who you're talking to?"

I almost shit in my pants when he asked me this as he was literally trying to put me in a corner. "Oh, I know who you are, Mr. Frank Munroe! License and registration, please."

"You think you're a huge, big shot right now pulling me over, don't you? Here, I hope this will not take long."

"Oh, I'll let you know, Frank. I suggest you turn the truck off and get comfortable. I'll be back." I walked back to my cruiser and the thoughts of what I was going to do were swirling around in my mind. I sat there in a daze before I grabbed the radio to get back to Tom. *"Hey, Tom, can you send a few more cars, please. I feel I may need more backup."*

"Absolutely, Jack, I'm on it! Marylin should be there in about ten minutes."

"Alright, thank you." Shit, I knew I needed to get back to the situation, so I got out and headed back to the truck. This time my handgun was at my side as I wanted to be prepared for any quick actions they may take. But Marylin wasn't coming yet; the main street in front of the police station was as dead as any typical night but a bit odd for the day before the fourth of July. Frank rolled the window down as he started the truck.

"You pompous ass, didn't I say keep the truck off! Turn it off now and step out of it!"

He shut the truck off and as he opened the door, I saw the sheen of a blade on the side of his pants. I kept my cool as he got out, sizing him up. He was barely 5'1", and as I looked down upon him and his fake cowboy ass jeans and hat, as he walked to the back of the truck, I saw the shit-eating grin he had on his face. "You better wipe that grin off of your face."

As I faced him to the back end of my truck while I frisked him and took his knife away, I found a pistol in the back of his pants. But when I went to step back, it felt like I had backed into a brick wall. I stumbled and got to my feet quickly, but Frank was now facing me, standing next to what appeared to be his security. "I said back off, big guy! I promise you'll be next!"

"Can I ask what your name is? I mean it's only polite as you already knew my name," Frank had said.

"My name is Chief Donaldson! Now turn around so I can read you your rights."

I went for my cuffs as I had one of his arms, but he jerked it around, catching me off guard. I stumbled back and slammed my back hard against the back door to the Bronco. I still held onto his arm and by now he was getting meaner and stronger; I knew I needed to take him down. I quickly hit him firmly in the waist, and just when I thought I had him, he jumped backwards, and I fell to the ground. We were both down but as he caught his second wind and stood, I went to follow. As I did, a throbbing pain shot through my ankle.

I couldn't feel my ankle and didn't have the strength to stand. I knew this wasn't a good situation. He and his friend stood over me as Frank kicked my side with his steel-toed boots. I was trying to catch my breath when his friend pulled his gun out and kneeled on my what now felt like broken ankle. He then leaned forward and put the gun upside my head and whispered to me the words that will be etched in my brain for years to come. *"Give me a good reason why I shouldn't pull this fucking trigger right now, you stupid fucking cop?"* His eyes were locked with mine as he hovered over me with the gun still drawn and Frank now by his side as I yelled in pain. He was the ugliest looking mother fucker with scars on his cheeks and a thick mustache which made him look even meaner.

"Come on, Chris, we can't be killing police. It's not Idaho. Besides, his buddies could be pulling up right now."

"You're fucking lucky my boss is making a great point. I'm going to spare your life for now." Just then there were high beams and lights on from the front of the truck and then in the back as Marylin had just shown in time with another backup. Tommy came over and helped me to my feet as I looked at Frank and his partner Chris. As I read them their rights, Frank asked me the most ridiculous question.

"What are you guys even arresting us for? You have nothing!"

"You're under arrest for the attempted theft of the sheep in the back of your truck. I should ask you, where were you guys taking them?" Marylin looked over at me, waiting for me to give up. I hadn't wanted to, but my ankle needed attention. "Take them away!" After my two other patrolmen had taken them away, it was Tommy, Marylin, and I left.

"Jack, you need to go to the hospital," Tommy had insisted.

"I want to take the sheep back."

"Jack, you are in no shape to drive. Go with Marylin. I'll take care of getting the sheep back. As it is, we will need a tow for them and the truck."

"Fine, let's go to the emergency room. I think Ipswich is closer and quicker." I hobbled over to Marilyn's cruiser and hopped in. As we drove over to the next town, she started a conversation I was not expecting.

"So, Jack, how's the wife and the newborn treating you?"

"Fine. I'm hoping he continues to sleep through the night for my wife's sake. How's things with Derek?"

Before she spoke, I could see a grin on her face as she rolled down the window to let the beautiful night air in. I could smell the sweet smell of her perfume. I hadn't a clue what she wore, but it was starting to drive me nuts. As I thought about this and what was happening, I hadn't realized she was mid-sentence. "— beers by yourself," is all that I heard.

"I'm sorry, I was zoned out for a minute. Can you repeat that sentence?" I felt myself getting red in the face as I felt caught like a deer in headlights.

"I was saying one of these nights you need to get out for a few beers. I mean, you do deserve a time or two for yourself. To answer your question my favorite chief, Derek and I are all done. He had left me for another younger woman about two months ago."

"Sure, I will keep that in mind. Thank you for the advice. Wait, two months ago? How come you're just telling me this now?" Shocked she hadn't told me this as we were somewhat close.

She giggled, "Oh please, Jack. You know well why I didn't tell you. It's that wife of yours that's always breathing down my neck with thoughts that I'm always riding your fucking cock.

Before I could answer we pulled into the emergency room front entrance, I was surprised to see my wife awaiting my arrival at the entrance. "Why did you have to call my wife? You know we have a newborn at home."

"Jack, she needed to know what's going on."

"She will be worried and all over my shit now."

"I will take that as a thank you." She smirked and brushed me off.

My wife was a bit of a nervous wreck whenever I went to work as she always said that we never knew what a day would bring. Even after the time I spent on the force with all the boring calls and no action, she still had concerns. She was looking for the one moment to jump on to have me reconsider my career. However, she was even sexier when she worried with her tiny five-foot frame and a tight ass that if I had my way, we'd be having back-to-back babies, so I was looking forward to some extra comfort when we were alone in the hospital.

"Oh my god, Jack, are you ok?"

I looked at Marylin with a shit-eating grin. Just then, Marylin knew I would be in trouble when I returned to work. "Yes, I will be fine. I think I just turned my ankle the wrong way."

As I hopped out of the car and into a wheelchair, my wife started to push me into the empty emergency room. This was an advantage in this small town of Ipswich, they had an emergency room in hopes of getting some overflow from the bigger city hospitals, but it wasn't happening yet. After we checked in, my wife pushed me over to the waiting area and sat with me, looking at me teary eyed.

"Why do you have to cry now, Alexis? I will be fine and more than likely going back to work tomorrow."

"Jack, you're so bullheaded and set in your Virgo ways. Can't a girl just sit here and shed some tears for her husband that risks his life day after day. The hell you're going back tomorrow!"

"We will see what they say, darling."

She had been perturbed by what I just said as she knew that the doctor would say anything for me to get my ass back to work. But she had a heart and was full of love. She held my hand until they called me in, and when they did, I felt her tiny five-foot frame struggle as she walked the wheelchair into the room as I loved to watch her in the reflection of the glass as it was that bright inside. She wasn't like most women. She told it how it was, and if you didn't like it then she would tell you there's the fucking door. She had a backbone and taught me to have one over the years. When she sat on the bed while we awaited the doctor, she was still dressed in her tight little sleep shorts that showed her ass cheeks and a hot little tank top. She was a tiny in shape woman all in a dynamite small package which I adored. Her eyes as she looked at me right then were crystal blue, like warm tropical water. They went well with her sexy smile that always got me weak in my knees. But the best part as I stared at her, was admiring her long luscious blonde hair that she always wore up at night in a clip to get my motor running.

"Jack, are you even listening to me?"

I knew I was caught not listening, but I knew a trick. I smiled before I answered her, "No, I'm sorry, I was actually admiring your beauty, Alexis."

"I was trying to say—" Just then the doctor came in to say he'd like to take some x-rays of my ankle to make sure there wasn't anything broken. "Jack, when you come back, I will tell you again what I was saying." I nodded as they wheeled me out of the room and down to their x-ray room.

The nurse was gentle as she helped me get into position to take the best picture of my ankle, and just like that, they were wheeling me back. The only downfall about a slow hospital was how quickly they could bring you back to your wife who is about to have an uncomfortable conversation.

"Here you go, Mr. Donaldson. They should be down shortly with the results."

"Thank you, nurse." I watched and waited for the nurse to leave as I turned to Alexis then, "so, Alexis, my apologies. What were you trying to tell me before we got interrupted?"

"Uh huh, I know your stall tactics, honey. I was trying to suggest you take some time off. It would be nice to have you home while you recover with whatever is going on. What the hell happened out there tonight?"

"Some shit with stolen sheep from Bothways Farm. They caught me by surprise."

"Don't ignore the first part of my conversation." She didn't really want me around, but she tried to be the all-around loving wife.

I threw her a smile even though she wasn't pleased by it at this time. "Ok, sorry. Honey, work needs me right now more than other times with this shit that just dropped in town tonight. This could be huge for our department with a lot of publicity."

She was trying to read me to see if I was twisting the story. She was usually cautious with this part, knowing I may not be divulging everything to her. She knew I couldn't go into detail much; it was obviously an open investigation. She looked perplexed with her thoughts as she thoughtfully came out with an answer I was surprised with.

"Ok, so here's how it's going to go, Jack. When the doctor comes back with your results to your x-ray, if it shows it's broken then you must be out until it heals."

Just then I saw my opening to take her statement one step further. "Ok, if it shows less than broken, meaning a tweak or a sprain, then I'm heading back to work!"

She looked like she was about to get mad as she was getting red in the face but decided I did beat her at her game, so she smiled her sexy smile towards me. "Yes, I suppose you have me there, Jack. I agree with this."

"Great. How was Jerry today?"

Before she could answer, the nurse came in to chat with us. She gave me a wink on the way in and I had a great feeling about this. When she put the x-ray up, the doctor followed in as he looked at me and then looked over at Alexis and gave her a very distinctive seducing smile. He was casually dressed, and his arms were showing with his muscle but also his tattoos. It made my blood boil seeing it; she was all flushed over herself seeing him and his tattoos. Odd though as he had an Airforce tattoo as well as a reaper. As soon as I was going to give him hell, he started to turn and talk. Alexis couldn't take her eyes off this guy that seemed nothing special.

"So, Mr. Donaldson. How is the foot feeling now?"

"Pretty damn good."

"Can you stand without any issue?"

I prayed before I stood and as I stood up, I had little to no pain. "Yes sir, I can stand with little to no pain."

"This is a good sign. You don't have a broken ankle. You just rolled on it. You were lucky as it could've been worse. Do you have any questions?"

"Yes, can I go back to work?"

"You have no restrictions; you may go back to work."

Alexis was surprisingly not furious with this turn of events; she was too interested in the doctor. As he left, she turned her eyes to me. I thought for sure she was going to lay into me; I prepared myself. "That's great news, baby. Your foot is fine, and you can return to work. I can't believe it. Don't get me wrong, I'm happy you're ok and got the clear to go, but yeah." She stopped as she glanced out into the emergency room. Then I knew I was in trouble as she turned to me. "I'll be right back, darling."

"Where are you going? I'm waiting for my discharge paperwork."

"I've got to run to the bathroom, and if I find the nurse or doctor, I want to make sure you're safe to go back to work."

I knew she was up to no good, but I really wasn't in a position to do something about it as my foot really did trouble me. I wanted to check in with Marylin to see how things were after the arrest. "Hey Marylin, it's Jack."

"Jack, I wasn't expecting your call so quickly. How are you doing over there?"

"I'm well and got the clearance to come back to work. How's things down at the station with those guys?"

"I hate to be the bearer of bad news, Jack, but the feds came in a short while ago and took them into their custody."

"No, what the hell were they doing? No, never mind. I should've known that once we arrested him, they'd have their hands…. Marylin, I'll see you tomorrow." I hung up the phone as I was distracted by what I was seeing outside my room. It was Alexis, my wife, flirting with that doctor. I acted nonchalantly when she came back in to see me.

"Hey darling, did you get that chat with the doctor?"

"Yes, he gave me your paperwork and he assured me that you're in great health."

I wanted to say something right there, but my words wouldn't get past the back of my throat.

"Ok, great, Alexis. Can we leave now?"

"Sure, are you coming home with me?"

"No, I think it's best for me to get back at it tonight."

The whole fifteen-minute drive was pure silence. As we pulled into the station parking lot, Marylin was outside the door awaiting us. I reached over and kissed Alexis before I got out and as I watched her drive away, I looked at my watch and realized how late it was. "FUCK, I was at the hospital for three hours!"

I started to walk towards the station but got interrupted by a Lincoln town car that pulled up in the front. It was black with very dark-tinted windows which was kind of scary given it was now 1:30 in the morning. As I approached the car, the back window slowly rolled down. A woman's face peeked out from the darkness of the car. "Are you Jack Donaldson?"

"Yes, yes, I am. Can I help you with something?" I awaited her response as Marylin came down the stairs to be near for backup.

She had a gun sitting next to her on the seat; I caught a quick shimmer as the only other car out on the road passed by. "Yes, you can start by getting Frank out of the feds hands."

"I'm sorry I think you underestimate the feds and how impossible that can be."

"I don't think you know who I am. Let me say that I can be your worst nightmare for this tiny, small town you oversee on the police force. My name is Andrea Dombrowski and Frank is one of my employees. A huge part of my thriving business. Now, you don't have much time as I'm giving you until noon today to have him back to me."

She slid her window back up and the car drove away as Marylin was now hovering over my shoulder trying to eavesdrop. I knew she couldn't hear much as she pretended to be a few feet away waiting for me to turn around.

"That was a bit sketchy. What was that about?"

"A woman that has threatened me to get Frank out of custody so she can take him back with her."

"And?" She had doubt in me at this moment.

"And what?"

"Jack, I know you by now. You're not giving me the whole story."

"Well, I don't know, she threatened this town."

"Jack, you must report this to the feds. Aren't you reporting it to the feds?"

"Well, we technically saved the sheep before they were gone. Why would you be questioning me after all these years?"

"You're right Jack, but what will happen next if you let him walk? Do what you want, I know you will."

She walked back into the station and as she did, I noticed her walking. I stared at her ass as she was walking as if suddenly being drawn to her. I was behind her and almost tripped as I went into my office, turned on the light, and sat down. *Fuck, am I attracted to her? Yes, I am attracted to her but now is the wrong fucking time to be staring at her ass.* I found the fed's business card and gave them a call.

"Jack, you're on the line with Agent Collin. We have Frank here. I'm sorry we couldn't wait for you to be back from the hospital before we took him. I hope you don't mind."

"Uh, even though I kind of expected it, it's ridiculous that you scooped him up before I could be here to be ok with it but that's not the reason why I was calling. I need you to bring him back. There's been no charges filed with us on the stolen sheep incident tonight."

"What the fuck, Jack! I thought this was a given chance to bag this mother fucker! You're telling me some farm country man doesn't think it's morally right to charge him because the sheep were returned?!"

"Yup, indeed! I expect him back down in Essex by ten in the morning, please."

The line had gone quiet, so I took the opportunity to hang the phone up. I put my head in my hands, wondering what the fuck I just did. I then concluded I had done the right thing to protect this town. I shut my light out and said my goodbyes to my officers when Marylin stopped me. The scent of her perfume was driving me crazy as she stood face to face with me right now.

"Marylin, I was just getting ready to find you."

"Jack, please don't play coy with me. What is going down about this arrest tonight?"

I then smiled at her which loosened her up. "Well, I talked to the feds and told them we're not charging them. I told them to have them back in Essex by ten."

"Very good. I really wanted to punch them big time for coming in here the way they did."

Being curious and needing to know I looked at her getting angry, "How did they come in here?"

"Oh, like they owned the place and because I was not aware they were bullying they walked in and told me what they were doing and by the time I was about to fight them, they were gone."

"Don't worry about it, I know how they can steamroll over departments when they want the spotlight. I think I'm going for some coffee; do you want one?"

"Thanks Jack, that would be great, but I thought you weren't coming back until tomorrow?"

I looked at her with a warming smile, "Marylin, I'm glad to be here with you too." Being funny trying to get her to laugh and it worked, "I didn't want to go back home after the hospital; besides you need me here." She smiled at me as she warmly touched my hand.

Before I drove off, I sat there thinking of her and all the time she could've been flirting with me. Was she really flirting with me? *Fuck, Jack, stop drifting about this woman.*

I drove a few minutes before I decided to go home and check on things as I found my wife outside on the porch having some drinks while the baby was sleeping in its crib in the living room. We lived in a great house on a small dead-end street called Kings Court. It had wide open fields in the back of the house and literally one neighbor. It was always super quiet no matter the time of day, and with it being just about three in the morning, there wasn't a peep going on but the crickets chirping. Had she been waiting up for me or was there something on her mind? Either way, it may not be good. I turned the truck off and walked up to the porch where she now started a cigarette to help along the buzz she had going on.

"Jesus Christ, Alexis, have you been drinking since you got back?"

"Oh, Jack, lighten up. Yes, I have. I mean, you were supposed to come home safe."

"Fuck, can you not change the subject before you answer me this. Why are you drinking?"

She had a way with me when I was catching her up to no good. She would start charming me with her gorgeous smile and this moment was about to be the same. She had put out her cigarette slowly and stood up as she staggered over. Once in front of me, she put her arms around me and gripped my ass.

"I thought you liked it when I got liquored up, Jack."

I contemplated saying something about what I witnessed in the emergency room. I didn't want to ruin her mood for sex now, but I couldn't resist. "Alexis, we should…"

She started to kiss my neck a bit. "What should we do?"

"Alexis, we have..."

She led me inside and to the couch as she staggered in, barely missing tripping as she was almost passed out drunk when I finally pushed her off me. "What the FUCK! Why did you push me off you?" She was furious, and the alcohol was fueling it. Her eyes always turned a greenish blue when she was angry and right now, they looked more green than blue. "I know what it is, it's your fucking side kick at work! Is it Marylin!?"

"Can you keep your voice down! No, it had nothing to do with Marylin. If you must know what it is, I'll tell you. It's fucking three in the morning, and I must go back to work and not to mention you're drinking is fueling your sex urge! Oh, just letting you know I decided to go back to work to think about things so go to fucking bed! Sleep this off!"

"I understand, Jack!"

She stormed off to the bedroom and as soon as I went to follow her, she threw my pillows at me as she thought she was punishing me or something. I let her think she won at that point as she laid down and passed out. It was fine as I never enjoyed sleeping with her in the same bed when she was drunk. Besides, I needed to get coffee and head back to the station. The few only times I would try, she either snored the whole night or beat the fuck out of me. Without thinking about this I took a deep breath and headed back out as I grabbed the coffee and headed back to the station to make it for the remainder of the night.

Marylin was at my desk awaiting, "Hey, I thought you changed your mind on coming back."

Looking at her with fury, "Nope, I stupidly went home to check on Alexis."

She didn't even say a word as she knew it wasn't good, so she came and shut the door. She then turned to me and gave me a huge hug. She slowly reached down and squeezed my ass as I caught my breath, *"Oh, please don't be shy. I have been dying to feel your ass, Jack. I'm so very sorry if you had a rough night. I hope knowing this will make you feel better."*

Chapter 2

I found myself with my head on my desk first thing as I looked at the time it was eight in the morning when Marylin came in. "Hey sleepy head, I thought I was going to have to pour hot water on you or something." I looked around the office as I was so confused now, as I noticed my office blinds were all closed when I reached for my bottle of whiskey, I kept in my draw for tough days like these and poured myself a glass. "Jack, you know that will not help the day."

I lit a Winston to help smooth the morning drink after all that had happened last night, I had needed this. "Well Marylin aren't you the mother hen right now." She didn't look amused by that, "Oh, please don't take it the wrong way,

The drink and Winston had worked as I was cooled down and ready for what would be a long ass fucking day. I looked at Marylin after my last drag, "Let's do this! Hng here as I want to go check up on the farm. I'll be back in fifteen." I put on my badge and hit the road for the station. I passed by Bothways Farm and took a quick peek out in the open fields. I could see the sheep already back and grazing the pastures like there was nothing wrong. It felt great knowing the sheep were back without any issues on that front, until I pulled back into the station.

I pulled in around eight thirty and as I got out of my truck, I noticed the unmarked vehicle that was near the front entrance. I passed by it and peered in to see that an FBI hat was in the back window. Fury overtook me as I winged the front door open and marched to my office. When I opened it and put on the light, I almost shit myself with fear.

"Miss Dombrowski, what do I owe the honor of you fucking making me shit my pants? Why are you waiting for me in my office?"

"I would love to know why you're getting in now. Isn't it out of your routine?"

I looked at her after she said this. It was my routine, but how did she know this? A bit of anxiety and anger ran through my body at this moment. "Are you watching me?"

"I know a lot of people that I have a high interest in. Now, I saw the FBI in the building. Is this a first for this small pitiful department?" She looked at me like I was nothing and she was talking down to me. She knew she had me over my desk and fucking me felt good to her.

"Yes, it is a first for us to have the feds visit here with something that is as huge as this. I have a question for you. Why do you have an FBI hat in the back of your car?"

"Jack, you small-town chiefs are smart. You see, now that you asked the magical question, I can be blunt with you. So, I'm part of the bureau but they don't know that I'm on the bad side of things as what I do I make a lot of money."

"What do you do?"

"Oh, you will find out sooner rather than later if you're onboard."

"What do you mean by that?"

"Never mind about that Jack, where is Frank and his guy? I have a flight I've got to catch."

"You are such a—"

Just as I was going to be super nasty to her, Agent Collins came into the room with Frank and another gentleman. He was close to seven feet tall with broad muscular shoulders and tree trunks for arms and legs. He was packing a pistol on his back side. "Oh Jack, can you calm down so I can now introduce you to my security. His name is Jimmy, and this is Agent Collins. He is also part of my security team." My face turned from red to white then to green as this sudden twist of things made the top of my head blow off like a mountain that hasn't erupted for many years. I knew at that moment things were not right, and I wasn't sure if I could trust anyone.

"Very nice to see you again and very nice to meet you as well. Have a seat while I go get the paperwork from my lieutenant." I slowly shuffled out of a very tense atmosphere. I kept my cool as I made my way over to Marylin's desk.

"Hey, Jack, what can I do for you? Jack, are you ok? It looks like you're about to get sick?"

"I can't talk right now, Marylin, but can I get the release paperwork for Frank and his guy please?"

I knew once I got that to the surface, I was in store for something. "Sure, here it is. I worked on it early this morning." She even had a smile as she was handing it to me. Meanwhile, I heard a cough from behind me, and as I peeked around the back side of me, I saw Tommy standing in the station now.

"Tommy, what are you doing here right now?"

"I wanted to come down and thank you for helping me last night. What were you just talking about? Are you releasing that fucking asshole who tried to steal my sheep?"

I quickly escorted him right outside the building, so he didn't make any more of a scene. "Tommy, trust me on this, please. It's best that we release him. We got your sheep back!"

"You and I had a fucking scare of a lifetime and you're fucking releasing him! He should be put away for this and all that he has done in the past. It's not fair!"

"I need you to calm the fuck down right now! I need you to trust that it will be fine!

"Jack, do you promise? If you don't hold this promise, I will make your life a living hell! Trust me on that!"

"Sure, sure. I know you will as you always have made my life hell Tommy." It wasn't anything new that he yelled at me with displeasure, but I had to walk on eggshells at this point as he was a ticking timebomb.

Thankfully, he calmed down and left as I got myself back in to get these pricks out of my fucking town once and for all. I went into the office as Andrea was just standing. She had a big fat old smile on her face. "I assume that's the paperwork?"

"Yes, it's the paperwork. I need them to sign it." They both signed it and as Andrea was about to leave when Frank's guy was signing his, she said something that would have me thinking of later coming.

"Jack, if you're ever in my area of the great state of Wyoming, please make sure to give me a call. I'd love to see you off the job." She handed me her business card as she left. Next thing I knew, I had Fank and his guy bumping me out of the way and chuckling as they left my office. It was just Agent Collins and me at that moment. It was time for me to stick it to him a bit if I could. As I shut the door to the office and gestured to the agent to take a seat, he didn't look pleased, but an evil grin popped up.

"Agent Collins, how many of you fucking people are corrupt?"

"How dare you ask a fucking question like that? I will do some damage to your tiny, small dick force here if this keeps up. Do we have an understanding? Besides if you must know we believe that there is a corrupt person in your department that you should keep an eye out for."

I gave him the deadliest of looks. "Oh, I understand. It will not keep up, FOR NOW! GOOD FUCKING DAY, GET THE FUCK OUT OF MY OFFICE, YOU PIECE OF SHIT!"

"I'm sure I'll be in touch, Jack. One thing, if you only knew why I was part of this organization you may understand better. Enjoy the rest of your day."

At that moment, I felt my blood pressure shoot through the roof as I let out a shriek at the top of my lungs. How does he have the audacity to assume that I have a corrupt officer here. I knew everyone would be looking in the office and instead of looking out, I watched Andrea give Agent Collins an envelope. Agent Collins looked at me as he got into his vehicle and left. I stood there for what seemed like the longest of times as I didn't know what to make of what just happened. It was then that the door slowly creaked open as Marylin strolled in.

"Jack?"

"WHAT is it, Marylin?"

Marylin gently broke the news. "Two things. One, your wife is here, and the other is we need to go down to the marina as there was a call for us."

"Uh, damn. How long has Alexis been waiting for me and did she hear me blow my fucking lid?"

Marilyn then squinted her eyes as she said, "She was here for that, Jack. I will be waiting when you're done with her."

I turned to look at her and before I spoke, I gave her the eye that said I meant business before I came out with, "Just go ahead down there Marylin and see what's going on. Let me know if you need me."

She smiled then as she took great pleasure. "Ok, sounds like a plan Jack. I'll send your wife in."

Alexis came in and started talking like nothing was going on with me at all. "Hey Jack, I wanted to stop in before I headed home to see what you may want for dinner?"

She had our son which put a smile on my face. "Awe there's my little guy. Alexis, how's he doing today?"

Alexis looked sharp and well rested after getting shit faced last night, when she verified what I thought. "Jack you'll be happy to hear he's doing well. He slept well and had a good healthy breakfast."

"I'm not sure what time I'll be home but if you don't mind getting some takeout. Surprise me please Alexis with what you get."

She looked hesitant for a minute and then replied, "That's fine, can you tell me though, what's going on with you and Marylin?"

I was shocked to hear the words come out of her mouth as I looked at her disgusted. "Where is this coming from?"

She looked very intense at this moment. "You always have her around when I'm here and you have many late nights. What am I supposed to think? Do you and her have something going on?"

I was sick with anger at that point, but I didn't want her to see as I felt she was fishing for it. "Hunny, I'm sorry you're thinking this, but please don't forget we both have a job to do. She is my deputy and that's it."

I didn't really like that she smiled a bit as she said, "Well I guess I will have to believe you, but you know this job demands a lot of you and we have a child now, don't you think maybe you should…"

I stopped her right in her tracks before she could finish the sentence, "Alexis, I know where you're going with that and please not now. You know this is my pride serving this town. Before you go I want to be clear on one thing, if you EVER pull what you did last night, so help me FUCKING GOD!"

I smiled down at her as she smiled back half assed as I gave her a kiss and she left. It was odd; I hadn't known a time since we'd been together that she came to visit me. She usually kept her distance from here. I went outside to see which way she went, and it was just like I thought; she was headed toward Ipswich, the next town over. She thought I wouldn't be attentive, but she was wrong. However, I didn't want to throw up red flags yet as she had a sister that lived in that town, and she could be visiting her. Besides, I had enough on my plate with what had been transpiring here at work.

"Jack, Marylin is on the radio for you."

"Marylin, what's happening down there?"

"Jack, you must come down now and see this. You will not believe what was found."

"Alright, uh, I'll head down now."

I grabbed my keys and headed out. I was halfway across the causeway when I slowed to a near stop to look down river; a large group had gathered down at the marina. *This can't be fucking good. What the fuck is happening?* My mind raced as I got over there ten minutes later to what seemed like a whole neighborhood that had gathered to look at the ongoing events. I got out of my car and tried to maneuver through the crowd, but I was struggling to make it closer. Finally, I yelled at the top of my lungs, "IF PEOPLE DON'T CLEAR OUT OF THE FUCKING WAY RIGHT NOW, I WILL ARREST EVERY DAMN ONE OF YOU!" I never saw people move so fast; they all dispersed back into whatever crawl space they came from. They hovered by their front yards with all being nosy just wanting to see what the bad event was.

Marilyn was the first to greet me. "Well, Jack, you certainly know how to clear a crowd out."

"Yeah, well, there was no need for them to not allow emergency personnel in. What did you come into?"

She didn't have any words to describe what she saw. She nodded her head, and I followed her. "Here is what I found first on the scene, Jack."

I was confused. "Uh, ok. It's just a stash of fish."

She looked at me perturbed as she thought I would see through the trick. "Oh, but Jack, it's not just a stash of fish." She then picked one up that they must've sliced into and as she showed me the fish, she added, "Do you see what's in these? Jack, there is a monstrous number of pills in here."

"Ah fuck. This is certainly not good."

"Oh, there's more." My mouth was open after she said that as she pulled my hand towards a boat that was nearby. It was a mid-sized boat that had some decent wear to it and with the name on it, Cattle Up, I had a slight clue where or who this might involve. We stepped onto the boat and went into where the boat controls were. Inside was a dead body.

I shrieked, "Fuck, this is the guy who was traveling with Frank, his bodyguard. FUCK, FUCK FUCK!"

Marylin was cool and calm as she was carrying out her duties. "I've got the coroner's office coming down. I'll deal with this."

"Thanks, I've got to go make some calls and figure out what happened here."

As I sat in my vehicle, dazed at what had happened on our docks, I was watching Marylin as she picked up the fish and put it in a cooler, she had borrowed from one of the fishermen. Thankfully, our town was known for fishing and clamming, so we not only had the equipment we could use but we knew who would always been going in and out of here. I picked up the radio and called into the station, "Tommy, can you please get Agent Collins on the phone for me right now?"

"Sure, absolutely, Jack. Give me a minute."

He had me on hold for what seemed like an eternity until I gave a couple of clicks with the radio to let Tommy know I was still here. "Tommy, are you getting through?"

He was quick to respond, "Sorry Jack, I'm patching him over right now."

"Agent Collins, this is Jack from Essex PD. Can I ask you a few questions?"

He was an asshole like I thought he would have been after our previous meeting. "This better be good, Jack."

I was beyond pissed now. "Yeah, tell me why there's a dead body on a boat that has never been here before, and a bunch of fish stuffed with pills!?"

He snarked a wise comment, "I really haven't the slightest clue, Jack. Perhaps you should be investigating your townies up there in Hicksville."

He wasn't seeing through why I was calling him, so I had cut right to it, "No, I'm starting with you as the person that is dead is the bodyguard that was with Frank last night!"

There was a long pause before he answered. "Seriously?"

I couldn't hold my anger then. "Yes. I want some answers. Now!"

His voice was calm but to the point right then. "You can't demand anything from me, let alone those who work for Miss Andrea. I would suggest you start investigating the town."

He hung up before I could get any more words out of him. I threw the radio down in the Bronco out of pure frustration. Marylin looked over at me. She was starting to walk over when I turned the Bronco on, backed up, and drove away. Looking in my rear view, I saw her shaking her head. I knew I needed to keep cool at this moment, but how could I? Someone had come into my town and stirred up crap that was never here in the first place. I got back to the station, but before I could get into my office, Tom was awaiting me, and he looked anxious.

"What is it, Tom?"

Stuttering, he answered, "What happened out there? Marylin called to tell me you were in a bad mood. She said you left before she could get to you."

Shocked Marylin gave him a heads up, I quickly responded to him. "I'm fine, Tom. Can you get out of my way, please?" He didn't move and my patience was growing thin. "Tom, why are you still in my way? MOVE!"

He then moved out of my way, but before I could make it to my office, I heard, "What did you find out there, Jack?" Tom was persistent with knowing but I wasn't about to give anything to him until, I was sure.

I looked at him sternly. "Tom, you will know when I figure out what's going on. It's an active investigation."

"Ok, so what do I tell the reporters that have been calling the past hour?"

"Tom, are you that fucking stupid!? I just told you it's an active investigation!"

I then opened my door and walked in. As I turned on the light, I jumped out of my skin. Andrea was sitting there in the dark. Why was she here? Where was the security? I knew I'd soon find out. "Andrea, this is twice in one day you were able to come into my office and scare the fuck out of me! What do I owe this visit this time? I know it's not because we owe you anything."

She smiled while answering me, "Jack, I do apologize for scaring the crap out of you. I hope that you don't mind that I made myself comfortable as a woman in a tiny place like this." She skirted the first question I had as she was looking at me with judging eyes now. Not mean but seducing, judging, dark eyes. The look had me speechless and calmed for the time being.

I repeated what I had asked earlier with an anger on my face then, "Andrea, can I ask you what I can do for you?"

Sitting now with her bare legs in a miniskirt that had me partially distracted she smiled again while answering me. "Well, I think you know by now that I have a situation here in your tiny town."

I suddenly snapped out of the trance her sexy legs had on me when I gave her an angry response. "Yes, there's one that's happening right now with one of your men involved."

She then noticed I was admiring her as she started talking, "Well, I was wondering if there's any way, we can look the other way right now on this?"

Shaking my head in disbelief, I answered, "Are you asking for me to turn a cheek after this has been reported?"

She then slowly got up out of the chair and came face to face with me. She was smiling with her sexy bright red lipstick and as she got close to my ear, I could not only feel the soft warmth of her breath on my ear, but her perfume was wafting into my nose. It was a sexy smell, one that was luring me and making me weak in my knees. She paused as I was wondering where this was going, and I was thankful that nobody was around to see what was happening. She then started to whisper in my ear as I stared down at her sexy tight body.

"Now, Jack, I think we can figure something out. What do you think? I saw you checking out this luscious body of mine and believe me it has been a while since it has been ravaged. Can we make an arrangement?"

I was dumbfounded now. I was without a doubt getting turned on. What more could I come up with now? *"Uh, sure. Let me see what I can do."* It was the most stupid line I ever came up with and I was thinking how unfocused I was now because of this.

I felt her breath on my ear and neck when she responded with a grin, *"That's good, Jack. I love the sound of that."* She slowly backed away as she grabbed her purse and toyed with the curls in her hair. "Let me know when you conclude, Jack. Also, think of what would make you happy. I will look forward to hearing from you."

When she walked out, I still had weird feelings. A mix between butterflies and a deep twist in my gut like I got punched. My loins had really taken a hit as I had to sit in my chair until my hard on had gone down. The gut feeling was because I knew I had just gotten taken for a fool, but I knew what I had to do. Before I stood up from my chair, I got out a shot glass, and poured myself a shot of whiskey. I gulped it down as I watched her every step to her car. As she drove off, I called the coroner's office.

"City Coroner's office, this is Abby speaking. How can I help you?"

Abby was my old high school girlfriend and my first true love, so I was ecstatic that she answered the phone. *"Abby, this is Jack at Essex Police Department. I must ask, have you heard anything from the FBI about the body that we sent to you?"* I could tell she was hesitant to answer me as she probably had questions for me.

She sounded happy to hear from me. *"Hey, Jack, it's been a long time since you called me. Why don't you come down to see me in person and we can chat more?"*

I was grinning like a little giddy schoolboy when I answered her, *"Uh, I can come down now if that's ok?*

She responded in a sexy voice, *"See you soon."*

I hadn't the slightest idea why she would've been this way over the phone, but I knew I would soon find out. The only thing to do was to fly under the radar as Marylin would be busting my chops if she knew I was going to chat with my ex from high school. *Geesh, sometimes I think she is worse than my own wife for some reason.* She had some years working with me as we shared a lot about our lives, so she knew my past with Abby. Thankfully, she had gone home for the day, so I grabbed my keys and my gun and walked out. I had a strange feeling someone was watching me. I turned and there was Tom right up my ass before I could get out the door.

He asked the same question he always did when I was leaving, "Sir, how long will you be out for?"

But I didn't really want to respond to him with the truth as I knew he was being nosey. "Why?"

Until he dropped on me a name that I needed to hear now, "I have Jay Kutty coming in to see you in a bit."

Not showing my excitement, I responded calmly, "Oh, well why, Tom?"

Grinning at me he said, "Security detail up at his mansion next week as they are shooting a music video up there."

Not caring about that now, I surprised him next, "Tom, I have all the faith in the world you can deal with this. Besides, I think you're his number one fan. I'll catch you later."

His pissed off answer almost got me pissing my pants laughing, "Jack, that was totally unfair of you to say that and run."

I smiled and gave him a wave as I left. I mean, on one hand this was Jay Kutty and the only reason he moved to my town was because he trusts us to keep him protected. Jay was an infamous rap star, and he moved to our town five years ago. He would do anything for us as we would for him. I shook off fear that Tom would fuck that shit up as I knew he may, but I had one thought in mind and that was to take care of this body right now. The coroner's office was about a twenty-minute drive south at the nearest hospital in a city called Beverly. Abby was on the other side of things; it would be nice to see her as it has been about fifteen years since we'd last seen each other. As I thought about her more while I was driving the highway, I was getting those butterflies like the first day we met. She had beautiful shoulder length brown hair, full and lustrous to match her brown eyes that made me melt like chocolate every time we were together. She had a smile that would light up any room on any given day. As I was in deep thought, I rolled into the hospital without knowing that I was there already. Before I got out, I thought of those adventures we had and missed those as I looked down at my finger at my wedding band. *What are these strange thoughts? She is a friend now and nothing else.* I thought of the way we broke up; it was over something stupid I put her through. I thought she was smothering me when I was in the military, I treated her so poorly until she gave up on me one day. Before I could get too far deep into that, I pulled myself out of it and headed inside the hospital. The office was in the basement and as I made my way through the quiet halls down to her place of work, I felt the butterflies even more. I knocked on the door ever so slightly.

I heard her sweet seductive voice say, "Come in."

Smiling with hearing that I quickly came out with, "Abby, it's me."

When she responded my heart jumped through my chest as it sounded like she was looking forward to this, "Come in, Jack." She went in for a hug. It felt great to see and feel her again.

She paid no attention to my warmth at the moment as she wanted to get down to business. "So, I could sense some tenseness when you called. What's going on with this? I know there's some story behind this."

I wasn't sure how I'd answer her now, but looking at her eyes I couldn't think, and words just spilled out of my mouth. "Abby, well, it was a quick investigation. I know who it was, but I can't really bring charges against her."

Confused with what I had said she asked the only thing she could, "Why?"

"It's hard to explain. She's powerful to start out with as she could keep bringing this shit storm stuff to our small town. The other is that if I'm able to rule this a boating or fishing accident, then she will go away for good."

"I see. I don't certainly want something to happen in our town. But before I'm able to do this for you, can you do something for me?"

Just then she put down her folder and came up close to me. "What can I do for you, Abby?"

"Let's meet for drinks one night when you have to work late."

I didn't know what to do. It felt awkward as I wasn't expecting this; she was the one who broke things off with us after high school. "Abby, you know I would love to—"

Before she could let me finish, she replied, "Great, meet me tonight at the tavern right across the line into Gloucester. Oh, if you were going to say your married, I've never liked your wife."

"Uh, sure. I thought you were living in Essex?"

"Nope, I'm about a half mile from Wingaersheek Beach."

"Great, I'll see you at ten. But before I go, can you tell me how he died?"

She looked intrigued to answer me when she came out with something I wasn't expecting. "Well, from what I could see he has a gunshot wound to his stomach, but I really don't believe it was an instant death for this poor guy. He had cocaine in his system as well as blunt force trauma to his chest."

"What exactly do you mean? Are you saying whoever did this made him suffer by bleeding him out?"

She looked perplexed before answering me. "Yes, that's exactly what I mean. I also want to mention that he had wrist wounds that indicates he was tied down after as well."

"Thank you for the information. Can you tell me how long it took before he had died?"

She was sour faced then as if I had touched a sore subject, "He didn't die quick, this person took the time to torture this person in many ways. Pick the poison, cutting off circulation of wrists or being strangled enough to think your dead but only come back with numerous kicks to the stomach as well as thin slices to the wrists for a slow bleed."

I was appalled to hear this, "FUCK! This is not good! I appreciate you giving me this info Abby. I should be heading out though for now."

"Jack, please be careful with this one. This is something I have never worked on before." She was always sweet and sincere with me.

What could I say as she was so sexy when she showed passion for me. "I promise I will, Abby."

When I was leaving, maybe I should have had a bad feeling in the pit of my stomach. I should have just gone to get what I was looking for, but I didn't. I didn't know what my plan was beyond getting that murder undone. What was I to do with Abby tonight? I started to drive away, and Abby was on my mind all the way back to the department. The information she gave to me though was credible about who I thought it may have been and the possible motive, but I also thought it could be a distraction to who it very well could be. What if the serial killer was sending a message to me. I knew I needed to keep it under wrap. When I got back, I had another unexpected visitor. Marylin was waiting for me in my office.

"Marylin, I thought I wasn't going to see you until tomorrow morning. What's going on?"

I knew she had information as her face said it all. "Well, I was heading back home just now when I saw your wife's car over at Ipswich hospital. Is everything ok?"

"Yes, of course. Why wouldn't it be?"

"Well, she is up at the hospital in Ipswich. Jack, you know you can always come to me if you need me. That is, you know, including marital issues." I smiled and as I did, I must've been blushing as she picked up on it. "Oh my god, Jack. I'm sorry if you're having marital issues."

I gulped before admitting this to the person who had been flirting with me since day one. "That's ok, thank you for asking."

She then put her hand on my arm, "Well, perhaps you'd like to come over tonight for a drink or two and chat?"

I looked away at that point as I was up in my head yelling, *Seriously all in the same night?* "That sounds like it would be great, but can I take a rain check?"

"I suppose, but if you change your mind then give me a call, no matter what time it is."

She walked out of my office. I was already feeling warm all over from my visit with Abby, but I then wanted to make sure I gave Andrea a call to let her know things are taken care of. "Jack, my darling, tell me you've got good news."

"Hi Andrea, yes, I do. Well, not good news but great news. I officially chatted with the coroner's office and told them I ruled it an accident while out fishing." It really wasn't a lie as I was going to make it official on that in the morning.

She responded quickly and anxiously, "I don't need to hear more, but I want to hear it, Jack. Can you tell me what the accident was? You know, just in case your crew comes knocking."

I smirked as I knew she'd feel this way, so I told her what she wanted to hear. "Ah, sure. The accident was caused by a fishing line that was caught on something and when the guy was trying to entangle it, his gun went off, shooting him fatally."

"Smart thinking, Jack. So, things are now settled there and I'm happy. Now, I want to meet you this evening to make it up to you. Meet me at the Skipper's Galley for some appetizers and drinks at six. Oh, and Jack, you will want to be on time. Bye for now." She was a businesswoman who wanted her connections to run deep, but I hadn't known how deep let alone how deep I'd get myself into.

She hung up before I could tell her I had other plans. I mean, I could tell Abby I'd be a bit later, but then what was I supposed to do about Alexis? It was already four in the afternoon, and I was having her pick up food for us. *She will understand; I will call her right before I leave to meet Andrea.*

Chapter 3

"Jack, I got you a burger dinner plate from Essex House of Pizza. I hope you'll like it."

"Yeah sure, that's fine with me, Alexis. I was calling because I will be working late this evening as I must wrap up some huge things that happened today."

"Jack, are you shitting me? You've been gone for like twenty-two out of the past twenty-four hours! I mean, Jerry is missing his father. He needs his dad."

"Alexis, did you see the news?"

"No, what's going on?"

"There was a dead body that was found at the marina today. I have some more leg work and then paperwork to wrap up before I come home."

"What the fuck! Was there foul play? Can you tell me anything about this?"

I had a feeling in my stomach that I was heading into a lie with her, and it wasn't feeling quite good. *"No, it wasn't foul play. It was a fishing accident. I will see you later after I get this shit done."*

I hadn't given her a chance to keep the conversation going as I hung up on her before I could even hear the I love you. I sat there thinking what Andrea could want. I went to my Bronco and got out my spare change of clothes that I usually keep for these circumstances. I changed into jeans and a tee shirt, and as I was about to call Abby, Tom came into the office to let me know Abby had called and left a message that she is able to meet for drinks around ten now. This was perfect timing as it should give me enough time with Andrea.

I walked back out to my vehicle and as I sat inside, I looked over the marsh beyond city hall and the baseball fields. It was around five thirty in shadowy daylight and as I looked, I caught a glimpse of a person lurking out in the marshland. I went out to see if I could get a better view and saw they were wearing black pants and a black hoodie. The hood was up to cover his face while he was walking through there. I wanted to go see what it may have been, but time was limited, so I hopped back into the Bronco to start it up. Suddenly, I felt a hand on my shoulder.

"Who the fuck is there!?"

"Calm down, Mr. Donaldson. It's Harry from the local paper. I've been trying to get a one on one with you for a few days and you're a hard person to get a hold of."

"Don't tell me to calm down when you're trespassing and breaking and entering a police vehicle. What do you want to know, Harry?" Harry was one of the best reporters in the area at the small paper out of Salem. He brought the truth even if it hurt people, and he didn't care what he had to do to get that information.

"I wanted to find out whatever happened down at the marina earlier?"

"Harry, all that I can tell you is it was an unfortunate fishing accident with an unknown individual."

He didn't look pleased with my answer, "Anything else you can tell me?"

"No further comment on this, Harry. Now get out of my vehicle before I arrest you for trespassing."

"Alright, alright. I hope you have a great evening, Jack. Thank you."

I drove off as he was still writing in his small notepad. I could've walked to the restaurant as Skipper's Galley was literally two minutes away, but it was super humid out and just in case there was a call, I would have my vehicle as there was really no time off for me. When I arrived, I saw a Cadillac parked out front that stood out. She was there already, and it was fifteen minutes early. I was screwed as I wanted to get a few drinks in me to loosen up before she arrived. I walked in and as they brought me to her table, she had a beautiful smile upon her face.

"Jack, have a seat. I hope you don't mind. I took the liberty of ordering you what I'm having."

"No, not at all. What am I drinking with you?" I smiled as I sat making myself as comfortable as possible.

She then winked and smiled at me. "It's straight up whiskey. I hope you'll catch up with me."

"Uh, how many are you on?" I was so scared to find out the answer to this.

"This is my fourth."

I knew I shouldn't, but I did indeed indulge. I wasn't prepared for this and maybe I should've; I was sitting with a woman who was very stunning and as far as I knew she was a criminal of some sorts, but I didn't care now as I was just sitting for drinks with her. I did indeed finally catch her as she was on her sixth and I was surprised she wasn't as drunk as she should be. She was cute in her slim back skirt that really showed her curvaceous figure. She had her hair up in a ponytail which was yet another turn-on as that was one thing Alexis always did to get my motor going. I loved to see a sexy women's neck. Her eyes were trying to search deep inside me to see what or how much it would take to pay me back and I had shown that nothing was sparking my interest, I was playing ball. She then took a drink and as she licked her bright red lip-sticked lips, she had me in a crazy daze until she had taken off one of her heels to get my attention. I knew I was busted right then and there.

"Jack, are you still with me?"

"Oh sorry. I lost my attention."

"That's perfectly fine." She giggled after that as she was now rubbing my inner thigh with her nylon-covered toes. "Jack, I know it's close to nine now, but I was wondering if you'd like to go to my motel with me?"

I was being seduced and as much as I was trying to fight it, I was losing the battle. She had a way about her. She was sexy to go along with, knowing it was a power thing. "What makes you think I would like to do that?"

"Don't play coy with me Jack, I feel the sexual tension between us as much as you do. Besides me catching you checking out my neckline as well as my nylon feet I think we should go back there to chat for a bit."

What could I say as I knew I was busted at that moment. "You got me Andrea. I will go back to your motel for a few." Then we paid the check, I hopped into my vehicle and followed her to her motel. To my chagrin, it was the Essex Inn. As we arrived and I walked towards her room, I stopped to look out in the marsh. I thought I saw a flashlight way out there near the tree line. Nah, it couldn't have been the same guy. I stood there for another minute looking to see if I could see anything out of the ordinary until I heard Andrea open the door with a crack. "Jack, are you coming in?" I was on an alert watch as she asked me again. "Jack, what's wrong? I'm already naked for you."

I looked in to see her head peeking out and suddenly, she opened the door to show she was naked.

She hadn't a single piece of clothing on, and the impressive part was it only took less than a minute for her to get naked. She had beautiful skin that wanted to be touched as well as soft breasts and a shapely figure and a nice ass that got me turned on, but then I looked down at the wedding band that reminded me that I was married with a newborn. I then looked back over the marsh and as I did, I saw a light coming now in the middle of the marsh. But how? "Andrea, I'm going to have to take a rain check." I hopped in my Bronco and left. I didn't know what went over me at the time, but I kept trying to tell myself I made the right decision for myself as well as my marriage. I started to think about the person and the strange light out on the marsh as I was pulling up at the place where I was to meet Abby. She was already inside the bar. Well, this seemed like the night I wished I was the early one. I looked down at my watch and saw it was already ten past ten; I guess I was a bit late.

"Abby, I hope I didn't keep you waiting for long?"

"Nah, I literally just got here." She wasn't kidding as her drink had just been placed in front of her.

"I'll have what she's having, please. What are you having?"

"Rum and Coke." Ugh, I thought I was going to be toast after this night.

"Still my type of girl with those drinks. How's everything been for you, Abby?"

"Well, I'm still obviously working at the morgue, and it's been busy from the area. There's been a lot of murders coming through. Enough about me, how's your life going? I heard you and your wife just had a baby together."

"Yes, in fact we did. It's going."

"You don't sound too sure about that, Jack."

"It is." I wanted to change the subject before I got myself in heat. "Did you say a lot of murders?"

"Yes, it has been happening all over the area. First, it was Middleton and now a string of them in Beverly. It is what?"

"I've got to get going, Abby. Can we continue this another time, please? I do want to share with you about how my marriage is not going, but I need to get home right now."

Before I was able to get up, she leaned in and locked her lips with mine. I could feel her tongue slip into my mouth; it felt like it did back when we were in high school together. It made me get butterflies and I was not innocent as I was kissing back. Finally, after a minute of the tongue wrestling that was happening, I leaned out and looked at the beautiful woman she was and wished I hadn't shit to do let alone figuring out what Alexis was up to with her motif just yet. "Abby, I'll be in touch." I left her sitting at the bar, smiling, which gave me a warm feeling on the inside knowing she was thinking about me. She was the girl who would know work comes first, unlike Alexis all the time with her saying I should be home immediately after work. That's one of the things I loved about Abby, and I was frustrated that I had to leave her hanging. I was more at ease after the drive when I arrived home, and the house was dark and silent. I crept inside slowly and quietly not to wake the baby or Alexis but as I made it into our bedroom, I heard Alexis shift in bed.

"Jack, are you finally home?"

"Yeah, go back to sleep."

She was persistent, "What time is it?"

"Close to midnight."

I hopped into the bed and kissed her goodnight. I lay there first thinking of Abby and then Andrea. *I've got to pay close attention to what my wife is doing before I let anyone make a move on me.* I was in a home that saw many people cheating on each other. It was mainly my mother who cheated on my dad all the time. I was so young I hadn't known better to know what was going on, let alone tell him. So, I had a strict behavior when it came to cheating; I was trying to break the cycle that I was born in. But I hadn't had any evidence of Alexis cheating just yet even though there was something off with her. I had wished I would have to spend more time watching her and what she does. I realized it was almost one and I was wide awake from my thoughts, so I slid out of the bed and downstairs to have a glass of whiskey. I looked over the fields in the back of my home as I was drinking. I thought of the murders happening all around and why I hadn't heard about them yet? What could I do to be prepared? I finished the glass of whiskey and relaxed in my reclining chair as I fell asleep.

The next thing I knew I was awakened by the sun shining as morning came or at least I thought it was morning. But weirdly enough I wasn't in my reclining chair but on my front lawn. I couldn't believe I slept out here last night. I started to get up off the ground and walk into the house when I tripped and fell. I got up and looked down but there wasn't anything there. I went into the house and there was police tape up all around what was in the living room, but now it looked like a motel room, and when I peered into the room, I saw a lifeless body. I couldn't see the face which upset me as I was trying to see what was happening and then I woke myself up, drooling.

I was dreaming about a murder but of who? I suddenly realized it was morning as the sun was already up. It was still quiet in the house as I put my glasses on and looked at the time. Fuck! I was late as it was now ten in the morning! I raced to get my uniform on and as I looked around for Alexis and the baby, I didn't see either of them. So, I finished getting ready and went to grab some coffee in the kitchen. There, I found a note.

Jack, I took the baby over to my sister's. Until things subside with those murders that are going around, I will split my time between here and there.

This wasn't shocking as Alexis had blown things out of proportion before. She was at her sister's, but she didn't finish the note with I love you. I went to go check on her and the baby's clothes and as I looked in the closet, she had wiped out most of their belongings. It made me confused but pissed at the same time. Why did she do this without speaking to me? How did she find out about those murders in the area before I did? I wanted to call her and as I picked up the phone, I heard a voice.

"Hello? Jack?"

"Mandy, I was just about to call over there. What's happening with Alexis wanting to be there for now?"

"Calm down, Jack. She and the baby are fine. She just needed to be in a steady environment for now. Besides I think she felt the need to be here for me right now."

"Why? She doesn't trust that I will help her?"

"Jack, just give her some space right now."

Then she hung up on me. It was bullshit; I had a feeling in my gut that they were up to no good. Alexis's sister Mandy was never married and one of the biggest liars and whores that I'd ever known. Even on our wedding day she was in the coat room at the reception giving all three of my best men blowjobs. She was also the one that tried to make a play for me to join them, and if it wasn't for Alexis being there with me, she wouldn't have believed me. Mandy wasn't even her real name; it was short for Amanda. She also had drug issues in the past as she was always hung up on the wrong people, so I knew Alexis went over there for Mandy's safety. I didn't have time to dwell on it as I grabbed my keys and headed to work.

I got as far as the causeway when my two-way broke silence. *"Hey boss, I was wondering if you were up and at them yet?"* I had a bad feeling about this as Tom never bothered me on my way in before. But before I could answer him back, Andrea was behind me trying to flag me to stop. I pulled into the Skipper's Galley, and as she rolled down her window to show her gorgeous face, I was warmed to see her.

"Jack, what happened to you last night?"

"Andrea, I do apologize as I had some business to take care of."

She looked dissatisfied as she so wanted her hooks in me. "When can we pick up where we left off?"

I smiled at her while answering, "I will be in touch."

She winked at me, satisfied with my answer. "Ok, don't take too much time as I will be leaving soon to go home."

She rolled her window up and took off as I sat there for a minute to think of how it would've been if I stayed with her last night and fucked her brains out. Yeah, it would've felt great, but I did the right thing for now as I wanted to figure out the Alexis thing first. I finally made it to the station where Marylin was waiting for me at the door with someone she had just arrested.

It was only eleven and she had arrested someone early for a Thursday.

I whispered to her, "Hey, what's this one in for?"

She smiled as she answered, "He was pulled over for speeding and come to find out he has warrants out for his arrest in Wisconsin for assault and battery."

I had urgency in my voice as I said, "Ugh, good catch. Can you ask someone to book him, please? I've got something I need you to do for me."

She looked intrigued as she answered me. "Ok, I'll be right into your office to see what you need." She was gone for five minutes before she entered my office. "Ok, I'm here for you. What do you need?"

"Please shut my door as I don't want anyone else to hear this." As she shut my door, I closed my blinds to have a completely private conversation with her. "Can you do something for me, Marylin? It's personal and if you don't want to, I would understand."

She was on the edge of giving herself to me as she was putting on lipstick at that moment. She looked up at me with all her beauty and this gorgeous smile. "What is it, Jack?"

Hardly wanting to disappoint, I answered her gingerly with softness on my face, "First, Marylin, it's not what you're thinking. I'm not asking for sexual favors even though I think you're very beautiful. Alexis left this morning to spend time over at her sisters in

Ipswich and even though she said it's for her sister and safety, I have this gut feeling it's something else."

She smirked then. "And you want me to tail her when I can."

I smiled back. "Yes, seeing as you live near them on High Street, I thought you could do this for me."

She had one sexy eye on me. "What's in it for me?"

I put it bluntly to her right then. "Well, just saying if she is up to no good..." I then went up to her, put both my hands around her ass, looked at her in the eyes, and leaned in and kissed her on her plump lips for about ten seconds before I leaned back and unlocked myself. "Well, there will be some of this to look forward to."

I had no idea what she was thinking now as her face was as straight as the best poker player. "That sounds good, Jack. I've been waiting for this day to come. I'll start tonight."

I smiled as I knew this would get her to agree. "Thank you, Marylin. I'll look forward to your reporting to me on this. Please keep it private."

I watched her walk out of my office as she had a grin on her face like she was giddy, and I mean I was giddy along with anxiety about all that was about to happen. She hopped in her cruiser and left for the day. I hadn't known what she would find or if she would be able to, but I knew she was the right person for the job.

She was always thorough in all her work that she was given and with this being my wife and trying to find out if she was cheating, well she knew if this was happening that she would get a chance at riding my cock.

Chapter 4

Tom rushed in frantic, asking, "Jack, can you go up and visit Bobby?"

I looked at him with a glare. "Uh, sure. What is it now with him up there?"

"Not sure, but it sounded urgent."

I knew when Bobby called something had to be wrong. *But what could it be?* I thought deeply on the quick ride over to see him. I was hoping it had nothing to do with the murders in the surrounding area. When I got to the farm around one in the afternoon, it was weird as there were no animals out in the field. There weren't even any swans swimming in the quaint pond they had there for the livestock to get their water source from. I approached Bobby's house as he was out there to greet me.

He was angry as he said, "You're a tough man to get a hold of Jack."

I didn't care now as I gave it back to him. "Well, it hasn't exactly been quiet lately Bobby. What's going on?"

He calmed down a bit after we exchanged angered chat, "I needed to let you know that I had a friend that called me a few weeks ago and asked if he could come visit as he is an avid fisherman. He had heard about our parts having great places for that and he went down Apple Street one day to fish and when he came home, he said he hadn't liked that spot."

I looked at him weirdly as he was all over the place. "Uh, can you tell the story so I can understand why I'm out here?"

He took a deep breath and continued with what I thought was a calm chat. "I was getting to it, you fucking impatient prick. I pushed the envelope with why as I knew it was a great spot to fish and he eventually told me there was this weird person in a black hood that was stalking him as he was walking the brook. I was trying to get a hold of you yesterday to tell you this, but I couldn't. Meanwhile, my friend went off towards the marshland beyond city hall to try some fishing out this morning. He usually comes back before noon all the time and he hasn't returned yet."

I didn't want to upset him even more, so I acted calmly towards him. "Bobby, this is something you should've come down to the station to report yesterday."

He still was frantic. "Jack, do you think there might be something bad happening?"

"I honestly don't know. What's your friend's name?"

His head was down now, "Red."

I had a bad feeling about this situation in my stomach. I quickly got into my truck and as I was driving away, Bobby yelled, "PLEASE KEEP ME INFORMED!"

I drove down towards the marina and parked my Bronco. I played it low key as I walked down close to the water and hopped into my boat, and it felt like it was hours that I was perusing the coast line until it had become dark and I had looked at my watch and what was once an afternoon on the water became a dark evening now on the water. I perused more of the shoreline to see where this person might be off fishing with no luck. I was turning around when I caught a spot close to the marina where branches were a bit mangled. I pulled the boat over to it and as I grabbed my gun and stepped off the boat, I heard a loud moaning just off to my right. I moved quietly and quickly towards the noise. I peered around the thicket to see a man in his fifties having sex with this woman that looked like she was barely thirty. I didn't say anything at first as this was a first for me, but then I turned my flashlight on to them.

I startled him as he was full on inside this woman. "Hey, what the fuck, man! You can get in on this after I'm finished!"

"Essex PD, stop what you're doing immediately!"

I didn't mean to flash the light on the man's penis just then, but I was enjoying a look at the woman when he swung it out. "Seriously, you're interrupting my dirty hooker time!" He was still hard and swinging closer to me.

I smiled then. "Yeah, so fucking what? Turn around."

He burst out with the funniest line, "I can't until my erect penis calms the fuck down. I don't want it in a tree and besides what am I under arrest for?"

I answered him with a pleasured grin. "Indecent exposure. What's your name, sir?"

He didn't hold back. "Mac Johnson. You will not be able to keep me."

Curious on this as I had a feeling where he was going with this, I said, "Oh, why's that?"

He smiled. "You'll see. I also want my money from you."

Curiosity caught me in the moment as I asked, "Why is that?"

He blurted out, "Because I never came, you ruined it asshole!"

I laughed at him. "Asshole, if you do not pull your pants up right now, you will regret it."

He pushed me. "Oh yeah, what are you going to do? Suck my cock?"

I then had enough as I kicked him in the nuts as he bent over squealing like a little girl. I pulled his pants up after I handcuffed him as I walked him back to my boat. By the time I had put him on my boat and went back for the woman, she ran. She was running through the woods along the river in the pitch dark and as I chased her, I caught a glimpse of what really brought me out there in the corner of my eye. The light from the hooded person was off in the distance that distracted me, but I kept moving to try to catch her. Suddenly something hit me off my feet. I was out for a few minutes and when I came to, I saw the woman standing over me with my gun in her hand pointing it at my face.

She was shaking badly as she didn't want to get arrested. "I never wanted to come all the fucking way out here to fuck some random heehaw!"

I was dazed and confused. "What are you talking about, miss?"

"Just shut the fuck up! I don't want to kill you. But you've already seen my face and all of me. Maybe you'd like some of this?"

Just as she was unbuckling my pants while I was laying on the ground with my eyes closed, there was a sudden stop. I didn't feel her touch for a minute when suddenly, I heard a faint scream. I looked as she was dragged off into the bushes nearby. I then heard her gurgling and crying. I then flashed my light towards where it was coming from as I saw her bloodied body falling to the ground. I then heard feet pounding off into the distance, running away.

I grabbed my gun as I jumped up on my feet and searched the perimeter but couldn't see anyone or where they went off to with the dark of the trees that surrounded us. After I buckled my pants, I went over and found her lifeless body. She had her throat slashed and an instant death. Awful as she was, she was a beautiful woman with long beautiful black hair and a beautiful complexion to go along with her beautiful figure. I searched for her identity to my own chagrin. It was beside her and I looked to see what it said for a name. Hannah Jacobs, from Beverly, and she was only 28 years old, so fucking young! *This guy will have to explain when we get back to the station.* I got back to the boat and the guy passed out, more than likely drunk. As I took the boat slowly back to the marina, I had to radio the station about the crime scene.

"Hey, Tom, please let all responders be on call tonight. Please get Marylin down to the station as we have a crime scene we need to get to."

He nervously asked, "Ah, when sir?"

I boldly answered him. "Now, please. If she gives you any shit, tell her I will go wake her ass up myself."

I could now tell he had his nerves and feelings on guard with his brief response. "I will do so, sir."

Marylin was thankfully awaiting us as I got back to the marina. She was flashing the light to know it was her as I pulled the boat in and docked. Meanwhile, the guy I arrested was starting to laugh uncontrollably. "You guys will not be able to hold me for long, fucking pig pricks!" I didn't appreciate his outburst, so I harshly yanked at him and stood him up and then took him down as we met Marilyn then.

"So, Jack, what's happening with the guy out here? I mean for you to be that rough with him."

Suddenly the guy stepped in between us and as he tried to knock me in the water Marylin pulled on his back and took him down instantly. "I WOULD SUGGEST STAY THE FUCK DOWN! YOU NEED TO CALM DOWN ASSHOLE! BESIDES WHAT THE HELL IS YOUR PROBLEM!?"

Before he could answer I interrupted. "I caught him fucking some random hooker over in a secluded wooded area back up in the marsh."

Before Marylin could answer me, he yelled, "What are you bringing me in for, asshole?"

Marylin answered before I could, "Well, for starters, indecent exposure. The next would be attempted assault on an officer of the law!"

Just then the guy started to speak, "That charge will not stick, and I'll be out in an hour."

Before I could formally introduce Marylin to this guy, she got the introduction. "Who the fuck do you think you are?"

"I'm Mac Johnson, but most people know me as The Crusher. The ladies also call me the fly banana."

"The Crusher? What kind of nickname is that?"

"Well, baby, it's because I crush a lot of people who don't give my boss what she wants. You're not even going to ask on the other name?"

Marylin shook her head while looking at me as I winked and smirked at her. Then she asked what she couldn't take back, "Ok, I will amuse you, why are you called the fly banana?"

He made a desperate plea, "Unbuckle my pants baby and I'll show you."

Marylin laughed at his plea. "Seriously, your plea to me is to see your fucking penis! You have other fucking shit you need to worry about! Besides once you see one heehaws cock, you've seen them all. Their either too small or crooked as FUCK. SHUT THE FUCK UP NOW!"

I was dumbfounded at what he had just said and realized who he must be affiliated with, not to mention I wanted to forget seeing his penis, so I changed the subject, "Mr. Johnson, is your boss Andrea?"

"Boy, you don't miss a thing for a funny looking French man! HA."

Marylin then got him into her car and circled back to me. "Jack, why do you think Andrea is his boss?"

I hadn't wanted to give her anything at that moment, so I stalled her, "I'll see you back at the station and explain there. If he gets cockier, tell him we will charge him with the murder of the young lady out there."

She looked shocked. "Wait, murder?"

I gave her my cool calm look to keep her from freaking out. "We have a dead hooker about a mile away from where I found these two fucking around. I'll be back. I must now decide who I want to call to come in to help us."

She was glad to be the one booking him even though she was short. "Ok, don't worry. I'LL BOOK HIM!"

I knew she was pissed at me for not totally answering her questions, but I wanted to get back to the marina to see if I could see anything. I arrived and stepped out of my vehicle and as I paused, I grabbed my cigarettes to smoke one as I needed something to take the edge off. I stood there smoking and thinking of the whole situation. I knew I needed to at least get some help from the state police, so I threw my cigarette down and grabbed my radio. *"Tom, can you call this number please and patch the call over this, please."*

"Sure, ready for the number."

"484-6484"

It rang about three times as my heart was at my throat, but this call needed to be made first. *"Hello?"* Her voice was a bit tense as she picked up.

"Andrea, it's Jack. I hope it's ok if I called you at this late hour."

"Jack, of course. Did you change your mind?"

Smiling and blushing, I answered firmly, *"That's not what I was calling for. I've got one of your guys down at the station."*

She sounded adamant in her answer then. *"Ha, all my guys were accounted for after you left my hotel room. Thanks for making a lady get all hot and hang her out to dry."*

I ignored the come on. *"I think you better check on your men. I have a guy whose name is Mac and goes by the name of The Crusher."*

Pissed off now, she said, *"Fuck! What happened to him now?"*

"Indecent exposure as I could book him for fucking a prostitute in public."

"Oh, those charges will not stick." She sounded so confident and smug answering me.

Giving it back to her felt good. *"Yeah, but murder will, and perhaps attempted assault on an* officer. The young lady was murdered while I had him on the boat."

In her pissed off mood she was begging me, *"Are you fucking kidding me? Fuck me. Can you release him?"*

I couldn't stop myself on what came out next. "Sure, it will cost you though."

Relieved but hanging on to my demand, she asked, *"Name it and it's yours."*

Nervously, I responded, *"A hundred thousand dollars. You get that to me down at the marina and I will make sure he is released. I'm down here right now."*

"Jack, what is the money for? I mean, a hundred thousand dollars, what do you plan on doing with this?"

Even though it was none of her business I felt that she deserved an answer out of respect. *"To take care of my son and myself going into the future."*

"Oh, I'll be right there."

I paced back and forth with what I just decided. I never did this before, I mean thinking of taking money as a bribe to do anything, but I figured now was the best time. I mean, there wasn't murder since I'd been a police officer, and I figured why the fuck not? Maybe for once be able to take care of the baby and be a step ahead of Alexis if she is planning on leaving me. I walked around at the docks while I waited for her to get there, and as I was looking around, something caught my eye. It was a light off in the woods about twenty yards. I walked over slowly as it was going off and on, so I decided to pull my gun out just in case.

I slowly walked to where it was coming from and looked around at the spot; there was nothing. I must've circled that spot for a few minutes in hopes of finding something, but nothing came of it. I was slowly walking away when I heard a creaking of a branch off in the distance and rather than stop to observe it, picked up my pace. I got back to where the brush line met the pavement and the moment I stepped a foot out, a hand grabbed for me! I jumped out of the brush but when I looked back, I saw nothing, not a sole that could've done this. Andrea was just pulling in and that snapped me back into the current situation as I walked over to where she was parking.

Smiling now, she said, "Hello, Jack. It's nice to see you again. How are you doing?"

"I'd rather not talk about it."

"You should talk about it. You look like you've seen a ghost."

Though I shouldn't have, I opened up to her, "There was something out there in the woods I was just checking out. I saw nothing when I got out there but as I got back, I felt that something was following me and even tried to grab at my hand at the last minute."

"Oh, perhaps I can allow a few of my men when they get back tomorrow to assist you in the hunt?" I was flabbergasted by her offer and must've looked dumbfounded because she noticed I needed something to help me relax. "Jack, come here." I didn't move. I was still looking at her beauty, even without makeup or anything. I then thought of my wife; I hadn't seen her for a bit let alone heard from her. I was about to make the walk to my vehicle when Andrea stepped in front of me. "Where are you going?"

I looked down upon her beautiful face as she smiled at me. She unbuckled my pants, pulled them down, and kneeled in the moonlight. She was relieving the tension she had felt now with all of me inside her warm mouth. She felt amazing as she was slowly working me over and just when I thought she was done, she pushed my back up against my Bronco as she pulled down her sweatpants. I didn't know what to do as I'd not been with any other women since before I was seeing Alex. Andrea was working on me as my eyes were closed and I was thinking about all the fun moments in my life with Alexis and how I could just let this happen. Then suddenly Andrea slowed her hips down as she hopped off my cock, she made it clear that she was done as she was pulling her sweatpants up. She saw my eyes still shut so she glided my pants up and buckled my pants. "You can open your eyes now." I opened my eyes to see her standing in front of me with the best grin on her face.

As I was buckling up my pants I asked her, "What was that for, Andrea?"

Dumfounded by my question, she answered me with one, "What do you mean?"

"I should say why? I mean why like this when you know I'm married?"

She smiled and winked at me. "Jack, here is your cash. Do you really think I was going to come and give you cash in the middle of the night without getting something I wanted?"

I grinned then. "Fair enough."

"You act like you didn't enjoy that. I know I enjoyed every inch of it. Your wife is a lucky woman." She smiled after saying this to me.

"Can you tell me something?"

"Sure. I mean I can be as honest as I can with you, Jack, depending on how far we take our relationship."

"If I saw my wife flirting with a doctor the other night, do you think that there might be something with that?" Just then I knew what I leaked to her was bad.

She came in close to me and looked me in the eyes. "Oh, you are not experienced at this. Jack, if you think in your gut, it's true, then yes there's something to it."

She acted like she knew more than she led on to. "Andrea, do you know something I don't?"

"Good night, Jack. Thank you for tonight and I'll be in touch. I should see my guy back by the morning." She left without answering my question. She was mysterious in a way that was seductive, and she knew it. I put back on my hood and unzipped the bag. I peered inside, but it was more than one hundred thousand. A note had been taped to it.

I hope this is a great start to a great working relationship. You should have no shame in what we did tonight as I felt we both enjoyed it. I hope things blossom from here. I'm giving you three hundred thousand for your troubles and to make sure you are fully aware of how serious I am in our newfound friendship.

I stood there thinking of what she was insinuating but then I was thinking of her and how great she felt when we were together tonight.

I hopped back in and before I could think about calling in some help for the murder, the radio dispatch came through to me. *"Jack, I hope I'm not disturbing anything. I wanted to let you know that a state police unit will be here in an hour to assist you in getting the scene controlled."*

"Ok, thank you for taking the initiative to get that call done." I was grateful that I hadn't been the one calling it in.

I hoped it was the two women that I had enjoyed working with in detail last year in Manchester's bank robbery. They were very flirtatious even though

Tom was trying to scare off people as he was trying to get all the guys to believe they were a happily lesbian couple. I hadn't believed him from the start. I kept my distance as I knew my hands couldn't be tempted, but now, I did not know what my wife was doing when not home, so I would have to think differently. I went home after a quick trip to the station to grab my house keys and as I pulled in, I didn't see Alexis's car in our round-shaped driveway. I was sure she'd be home when I got home. I went inside and as soon as I turned on the lights, I saw a note on the living room table.

Jack, I never wanted to be away but here I am writing this letter to you to let you know what came to my decision. You're so fucking wrapped up in your work that it leaves no time for us! You always come home tired and not in the mood for talking let alone to fuck your own wife. I think we are growing distant as our own lives have done this. I'll be over my sister's indefinitely now until I can figure out what me and the baby will be doing.

I stared at the letter for a few minutes to try to read between the lines. The more I stared at it, the more pissed I got, so I balled it up and threw it down. I grabbed one of my shot glasses and poured myself a bourbon. I gulped it down and as I was thinking about the time I spent with Andrea and the passion that was there, I couldn't help but get more frustrated with my wife. I gulped down my second shot, grabbed my keys, and decided to go for a drive. I looked at my watch as it said it was almost two in the morning already. I drove until I reached her sister's street.

I crept up with only my fog lights on as I drove by her sister's home. I didn't see Alexis's car there. I looked around on the side streets and saw nothing. I was thinking of what Andrea was insisting to me with her read between the lines. *How did she know?* I went back towards the town I grew up in and loved all my life and found my way to the cemetery.

I pulled up in front of where my father was buried as I got out and walked over to have a chat with him, *"Dad, I hope you're listening. I have so much in the way of troubles, personal and professional. I could use some of your knowledge from when you were on the force on how to go about trying to capture this awful person by putting the scare to our citizens. Is it right if Alexis is cheating? Does it give me the right to do it as well? I mean, technically she came on to me."* The thoughts were that I was being ridiculous in my head and that cheating was cheating. But if she's cheating then why shouldn't I as if she is I would not want to be with her anymore.

Suddenly I heard something off in the distance, *"You, hey you."*

I heard a voice in the distance, a far distance in the dark, but I couldn't see who it was. "Yes?"

Then it was telling me a harsh reality, *"Snap the fuck out of it. Don't be a pussy. Your wife is not living with you; don't be harsh on yourself!"*

"Who are you? How do you know me and my life?" There was no answer back as I looked around at the darkness that was beyond the old graves that surrounded me. I then got back into the Bronco and as I was leaving, I flicked my high beams around to see if I could see anyone. There was nothing immediate that I could see, until I was outside of the cemetery and passing by an old house that I grew up in. There I saw in my rear view a person in a black hoodie. I slammed on my brakes and looked in my rear view again, but he was gone.

Chapter 5

When the sun rose at five in the morning, it had awoken me from my apparent drunken stupor at the night I had. I looked around after a minute of collecting myself and spotted my bottle of bourbon in the passenger seat. I had no recollection of even pulling it out. I then looked up out the front window to see the black-hooded person standing there in the middle of the street. I didn't know what to do at that moment as we stared back at each other, so I started my Bronco.

I was about to reverse it and call for backup when I looked at this person one more time. I revved the engine and put my foot heavy on the gas. I drove towards this person doing about 45 miles an hour before I realized what I was about to do. This person hit the front of my Bronco and flipped up on top of my vehicle and as I stopped to look back, I saw a person face down on the pavement. I got out of the vehicle, leaving it still running as I walked to get a closer look at what appeared to be the suspect. I turned over the body and I slowly pulled the hood down to reveal their identity. Who I saw made me sick to my stomach. It was Alexis's brother! *Why is Braden all the way over here? There's a lot that must be answered but first try to see if he is still alive.* "Braden, are you ok?"

"Jack, you mother fucker! Why would you do this to me? No, OH MY GOD, FUCK, I'm not ok."

"Stay with me so I can get you some medical help. First tell me why in the fuck are you over on this side of town?"

"OW! I'm in pa— pa— and you want to ask me questions?"

"Don't be like this, Braden." I looked down the road to see a black hooded person running off into the woods. When I looked down again, I was shocked. "Braden, oh no. Braden, please wake up. Braden!?"

He was semi-conscious then, *"Jack, I had been in the area camping out doing my thing. Please make the pain stop."*

"I'm trying Braden, just hold on. So, you're telling me you were using in the woods? You stupid mother fucker, do you know what you did here today? I ran you over thinking you were the hooded serial killer!

What were you doing out here anyway besides doing your thing in the woods?"

"I...I was run off the part of the woods near the marsh by some rough looking guys. Although they hooked me up with some fantastic drugs but only if I moved away from the area."

I was just now understanding why he came out of nowhere as I asked for more, "Braden, please answer me what those guys looked like?"

It was too late; just then he was unconscious. As I looked at him, I wondered if this was indeed a person that I wanted to save with all the crap he had put us through. I knelt over him, then decided to perform half-ass CPR on him until I knew it was too late and he was gone. I mean this fucking idiot could've had anyone thinking with his black hoodie out here in the woods that he was the serial killer and now that I knew he wasn't the killer, it didn't make me feel any better as it had me in a heap of shit. I knew he couldn't be the murderer, but he always had to conceal his identity. I was speechless as I looked at him trying to figure out why he'd be over here for the use of his favorite drug, Meth. Until I figured it out what and why. I was just looking down at him with sadness and anger right then.

I allowed my wife's brother to die at my own hands! I knew I couldn't call this in as I didn't want anyone to know my actions of driving someone over. I didn't have much time before the early morning risers came down to fish. I picked up his bloodied lifeless body and popped him in the back of my vehicle. I looked at him still with disbelief but not sadness. We hadn't seen him for months as he used to be one of those people who lived in the woods and hated civilization. He hated me when I married his sister and always took his aggression out on her and I. He used drugs and never had a place to live as he camped out in the woods and rode his bicycle around. Until one day we never heard from him again, and we both thought he just went somewhere warm or died. I did my best to search for him throughout the country but with not much luck. I quickly came out of my thoughts as I really thought it a huge relief to know we would not be putting up with his crap anymore. I mean, we tried to get him into rehab before he vanished, and he spit in our faces. But what was I going to do with his body? He still never deserved to die like this at my hands. I brought myself to lift his body in the back of the Bronco and started to drive away from the scene and back towards town, and I passed by the motel that Andrea was staying at. I was pulling in to see her when my radio scared the crap out of me.

Tom's voice was scraggly coming over the radio, *"JACK!"*

I laughed but gave him shit, *"YEAH! You should know better than to scare the crap out of me."*

He was brief as he didn't want to hear me scream anymore, *"Sorry about that. I wanted to let you know the state police are headed that way soon, and I'm patching over Alexis."*

I quickly got my calm voice going, *"Hey, how are you doing?"*

Nothing fazed her at this moment; her voice sounded cold. *"Fine, I wanted to let you know I'm grabbing some money, well my half, out of the bank today so I can get going."*

I was calm but wanted to get my question in before she wanted to hang up on me, *"Sure, take what you want. That's fine. I read your letter. How could you do it like this?"*

She was stone cold right then and I mean cold as if it wasn't snowing, I thought it could, *"Jack, you knew it was coming. Don't act surprised!"*

I lost my cool right then. *"Yeah, but you did it like this! I mean, if you want to act all innocent, I know what you're about to do with them too."* It was silent for a minute after that. *"HELLO, are you still there?"* There was nothing as she hung up the phone on me. She knew I was right as I sat there in front of the motel thinking about what had just transpired. She was cold and now I had my answer, my marriage was gone as I faced a very trying time in the town's history with drugs and murder in it. I needed to clear my mind to fix things and quick. Until I alerted myself out of my deep thoughts.

KNOCK, KNOCK, KNOCK. Andrea was right outside my door which scared the crap out of me. Just about pissing myself, I rolled down my window. "Hey, I was hoping you have a few minutes," I said.

"Sure, is everything ok?"

"Yeah, why?" I lied to her now as I didn't want anyone to hear what had just transpired.

Concerned as she opened my door, she said, "Please come into my room and talk to me, Jack."

We walked in and it was just her and I as she sat in the only chair in the room. "Please, make yourself comfortable." Of course, she gestured to the bed, and I sat without thinking. "Jack, I'm sorry but I was outside your vehicle for a part of that conversation. Are you ok?"

I was still not speaking the truth even as we were in the privacy of her room. "Yeah, why wouldn't I be?"

She was blunt then. "Oh, maybe your wife has left you and taken your baby?"

I loved that she shot from the hip like she did at this moment, "I'm fine."

She didn't push it but was firm that she was going to find out in her answer, "Ok, I'll come back to this. What can I do for you?"

She sat there in her sexy tiny half shirt and shorts as she crossed her legs in a way that let me know she had no underwear on. Distracted by this, I caught myself and cleared my throat to gather my thoughts. "Well, as you know, there is some random person going around murdering people and after you left me last night, I saw someone with a black hoodie. They disappeared after a few minutes and then I knew I woke up in my vehicle to the morning sun."

She had cut right to it, "So, what does that mean? Why you're here?"

"When I came to this morning, this person was staring me down and one thing led to another I decided to run him over. When I went to reveal this person's face, I was shocked to see who it was."

Shocked and interested, she played into my story. "Jack, who the hell was it?"

"It was my brother-in-law, Braden." She didn't flinch at what I had told her at this moment as I already knew that it was her men that came into contact with Braden.

She shrugged her shoulders. "So, what's the big issue?"

"I can't really call this one in as I don't want my wife to hear of how her brother died. I was hoping you knew of someone that had a way of disposing of the body?" I felt cheap when I asked that, but I had no other options as I knew my wife already had me by the balls.

She smiled as she asked me the all-important question, "Where's the body, Jack?"

"In the back of my vehicle." My head was down at that moment.

She opened the door and waved to a few of her people to come in. "You guys, this is Jack. He is our friend from the police. He has vowed to help us with our things. He needs us on this one. Loni, here's his keys. I want you two to take the body out of the back of his Bronco and clean it up but first take the body to Air. Tell him to transport it to our farm in Idaho; he should know what to do with it from there."

He nodded. "Yes, ma'am."

She shut the door and had a bit of a sexy grin as she shook her hips, walked over to the bed, and sat beside me. "See how easy that was. You asked me and I shall help you out."

"I very much appreciate it, Andrea. Can I ask when you say bring the body to Idaho, is that a safe place to dispose of it? Also are you able to bring me down to the station?"

She winked at me then, "Well, maybe in a few. To answer the other question, I will tell you that the place where your brother-in law is going, not one sole will find him there."

Just then there was a knock at the door. "One second." She opened it a crack and there was a whispered exchange that ended with Andrea shutting the door and turning to me, "Jack, you have a radio call right now that I think you may want to answer."

I looked at her weird as I got up and went out to the Bronco. "This is Jack, what do you need, Tom?"

I dropped the handheld the moment the words came out of Tom's mouth, "Jack, the state police were there on scene for the last hour and didn't recover any dead body."

I was relieved but angered at hearing this, so I didn't hold back, "What the fuck do you mean? It's gone?"

Scared, he squealed a few words. "Uh, yes, they searched the area and came up with nothing. No clues."

"HOW COME YOU DIDN'T INFORM ME THEY WERE THERE IN THE FIRST PLACE!?" Dead silence came from that before I asked, "Are they still there?"

He was confident in his answer, "No sir, they reported if there is any other sign of anything they will come back out."

"Don't bother me right now; I have some things to figure out!" My thoughts raced just then, *who moved that fucking body? I mean I didn't stay with the body because I thought it be safe until they got there. FUCK! This would be the one and only body that got away.* I walked back in where Andrea was awaiting me on the bed. All in her own sexiness waiting to hear what I had just been reported to about, and I must've been red in the face with anger as she was all over making me feel better.

"Jack, is everything ok?" She then peeked out the door to give her men the ok signal to take care of the dead body and cleaning up the Bronco. When she came back to bed and sat, she wanted to know what was going on. "Tell me what did you just hear? I know it was something as you're all red in the face."

Instead of answering her, I came out with a question to start, "Can you answer me something, did you send your guys out last night to take care of that body out there?"

Her smile got larger as she came face to face with me now. "Yes, my guys immediately went out there to the spot and took care of the mess that Mac left behind. Is that wrong?"

Just then before I could answer her, she put down her drink as she slowly straddled me with all 125 pounds of her. "What are you doing?" She ignored my question as she started to kiss me. As I leaned down on the bed and allowed it to happen, she took my pants off in no time as she grinded against me until she couldn't take it anymore. She pulled her shorts off to the side as I had my eyes closed. Then I felt the warmth of her as she was sliding down on me, bouncing up and down on me like a toy. When I opened my eyes to both of her hands firmly on my chest, I looked into her eyes, and they spoke to me. They told me to fear this woman but be fond of her. I felt her slowing down after a few minutes as she was quick to enjoy herself, then she slowly melted down towards me, still moving her hips until I was all orgasmed out. She stayed on me a few minutes as we were once again connected and I was becoming fond of this woman, even though I knew it was wrong and against my morals of a police officer and protector of this town. But it felt right in the moment as she slid off and laid right next to me with her hand on my chest. Then she asked me a question that I hadn't thought more about.

"Can I kiss you?"

I looked at her with a very serious look as I hadn't thought she was serious. "You can of course kiss me." She had very soft lips and tasted like strawberries and cream. "Why are you into me so much?"

"Jack, like I said last night, I think we both can help each other out. If it makes you feel any better, I think your wife is a stupid fucking bitch for whatever she's doing to you."

"That's so kind and I don't know where this is coming from as we really just met and this whole thing that you're doing to seduce me is so wrong."

"We may have just met but I see right into who you are. You're a sex deprived husband who does everything for his wife and kid and gets nothing in return. You also have a dark side which I haven't figured out yet and how deep it goes." I looked at her in silence and disbelief.

"You may be right on that, but I feel like I've never acted on those dark thoughts of being with another woman until now." I got up and started to get my clothes back on as I was getting offended by her comments.

"Jack, did I touch a sore spot? If I'm right, I'm not faulting you."

"No, you didn't touch a sore spot, I mean of course my dark spot is picturing myself with other women when I was with my wife. If you want to know the thing that's got me all pissed right now is you're avoiding more questions I may have and my frustration over your actions. I mean well yes you did touch a sore spot, I'm really a great guy I was trying to tell you. I am not the cheating type and you daggered me with comments to make me feel even worse!"

Her hands were square on her sexy hips at this moment as I could tell she was getting heated. "First of all, I never intended to make you feel that way. I'm glad we have this sexual attraction with a working relationship. Second really, what actions? Do you mean that I care enough to protect you from harm? Because I really don't think you're coming at me because I cleaned up a sex scene that was a murder sight! Perhaps envisioning all those women gave you courage enough when you finally realized your marriage is over you now don't give a fuck, you're going to fuck a sexy woman when you have a chance!"

"Care? Did you just say that word? I've got to go for now. I'll be in touch. Oh wait, one last thing, you're right, I now don't give a fuck about sex with you because yes, my marriage is over and having sex with you, well, again I'll be in touch." I was scared at the thought I was getting in too deep with a criminal and I would go down when she does.

Before I could shut the door, she came out with something I haven't heard for a while, "Make sure you are back in touch as I will miss those hands." I shut the door right then.

I needed to get back to the station, but with no vehicle, I thought better of it. Instead, I walked down to a breakfast nook nearby and got a cup of coffee as I read the newspaper. I saw the headline that was on the front page, and it was about the murder. *"Murder Upriver!"* I knew I was in trouble as the newspapers were already starting to get a hold of this. "

Dead woman found overnight as it looked like the Massachusetts murderer may soon be called a serial killer.

I was into another sip of coffee when a tap on my shoulder just about almost spilled it down my uniform.

"Hey, sorry to startle you, Jack. How are you doing? I wanted to see if you still wanted to get together with me soon?"

"Abby, oh my goodness. I'm doing alright. Well, as well as one can be with what's going on now. Yes, I would love to get together with you. Can we meetup for some drinks tonight?"

"That would be fabulous. I'll see you at our old spot."

As she gave me a sweet soft kiss on the cheek before she walked out, I thought of the old times she and I spent together drinking at our favorite place called Callahan's. That was a special spot to me with a lot of meaning as it was one of the first clam shacks in the town of Essex. After I'd get off work, she'd meet me for a night cap. I even once thought of proposing to Abby there on her birthday, before we grew distant.

"Jack, why don't you stay and have another?"

"Because I have to get up in about four hours to be back at work."

"Come on, please!"

"Ok, but you'll need to drive me back to your place. My parents would kill me coming home drunk like this."

"Jack, I will definitely take you back to my place."

"Jack? JACK?"

Suddenly, I was snapped from my memories. "Hey, Loni, what's happening? Sorry, just thinking of a lot."

"No worries, sir. I've come to let you know your vehicle is ready to roll."

"Excellent."

After a quick walk back, I got into my car. Before I could drive away, I saw Andrea from her motel door smiling, but I paid no attention as I had to get back to the station. I slid into and barely sat down at my desk when the state police were there without notice. I grabbed a coffee and went out to let them know where

I may need coverage. "So, Sergeant Dunsbury, I do deeply apologize for you and your department having to come down here for nothing."

"With all due respect, Jack, I wonder how something like that could happen. I mean I was going to let this go but it had bothered me about why this scene wasn't controlled more if there was a dead body out there?"

I was anxious now and very desperate to skirt this situation. "What will it take to overlook this?"

He looked calm when I had asked this as he had something in mind. "Oh Jack, I will not push this one; I really just wanted to come bust your balls." He smiled at me right then as I calmed down until he got up to my ear and said something that I never wanted to hear, "If this does happen again, I will come down like a vengeance. Do you understand me?"

The bastard just walked away before I could even get into any more words with him. Marylin walked over then. "What was that all about?"

"Ah, he was just flexing his ball-busting skills over how we handled this body at the marsh missing."

Her genuine self-had come through in her reply, "I'm sorry, Jack, but getting that is just utter bullshit! We slave every day in this town to have it as safe as it is!"

"Thanks, Marylin, I appreciate that. It's fine, I can handle a little ribbing and God knows I deserve it after this one. I'm going to take off for the rest of the day. Do you think you can cover, please?"

She looked at me concerned right then. "Jack, is everything ok? This isn't like you to just take the day off."

I didn't hold back as I knew she read me like a book, "Alexis is moving on without me. Before you ask, I just need some time to adjust to it."

I walked away as the state police were just driving off and leaving the station. I thought about the dead body being moved and the scene being cleaned. I felt like I needed to let it go as this trouble has somewhat been avoided as I knew the residents didn't need to hear of this body. But did I need to thank Andrea? I knew there was one in order, and I almost turned to see her when I stopped myself with thoughts of getting myself ready to see Abby later. I knew if I stopped to see Andrea it would lead to a long sweaty sex session in which I hadn't it in me again today. I got home and when I approached my door there was a note knifed to the door:

This is a statement to the police of Essex, you and your people in this town are warned that this is just the start!

I was about to call the station to let Marylin know, but if I wanted my privacy with Abby tonight I shouldn't as Marylin would be at my house instantly to detail it to make sure I was doing good. I got a very bad feeling about this note, but there wasn't anything I could do as I really needed a bit of time today with the Alexis situation going on. Damn, Alexis was still toying with my mind and emotions. Why should I feel this way as she left me! I shook it off as I started to look forward to seeing Abby as I popped open a Miller Lite and went in for a shower. I was enjoying the warmth of the water when I heard the phone ring. I let the answering machine snag the call so I could have a few extra minutes soaking my head. I had thoughts of how I wanted it to go with Abby and I was getting a bit excited thinking about it. It could go many ways and none of them were bad. I finally got out of the shower and went to check the message, *"Jack, it's Marylin, I wanted to check in with you to see how you're doing and if you needed anything. Please call me back and let me know."*

I picked up the phone with a smile, *"Marylin, it's Jack. You don't need to check up on me. I'm fine and will be fine."*

She had excitement in her voice, *"Jack, I'm glad to hear. Would you like me to get anything for you and bring it by?"*

I turned her down easily as I knew what that meant for her to come by, *"Oh Marylin, that's sweet of you but I will be fine. I'm going to probably go to bed early as I will be back tomorrow. I promise I'm fine though. I will take a raincheck on that though."*

She was empty with her answer right then, *"Oh, ok. I figured I would offer...."* I hung up the phone as I didn't want to hear her sadness as I was excited to be meeting up with Abby.

Chapter 6

After I got off the phone with Marylin I went and put a pair of jeans and a tee on this warm and humid July day. I grabbed myself a beer and sat at my country style kitchen table. I was drinking as I stared off out of the window just listening to the birds on the quiet day and thinking where it could have gone wrong in my marriage. I always thought it was my working sometimes around the clock or maybe perhaps it was hunting season when I was gone for days on end. I used to go out for afternoons to hunt in deer season in hopes to get a decent food storage which come to find out she didn't even like deer meat.

Nah, it was neither of these. The more I thought about it, the more it came to me. She was tired of the marriage; I truly think she fell out of love with me. The more I thought about it, the angrier I got as I spent the past five years that we were together trying to please her to the ends of the earth. I slammed down the beer and stood by my sink overlooking the backyard. There was a greenish haze out there this afternoon, and it seemed like it was growing. As I put on the news for the weather, I hoped that there was no severe weather moving in, and as I turned on Channel 5 News, sure enough, Richard Albert was giving his warning for thunderstorms later that evening. I ignored it as I was really looking forward to seeing Abby today. *I mean, hell, if Alexis can do this to me and call it over, I can certainly see other women.*

I found myself ready in a nice pair of jeans and a tee shirt that was showing off how in shape I had gotten over time since the last time Abby and I were together. I felt good for the time being knowing I was going on a new adventure and meeting not just someone different but someone I knew that I felt there was still a huge electric connection.

I made it to the place Abby had mentioned around five thirty, Callahan's, a place that had been in eastern Essex for the longest time with neighboring Gloucester only seconds away. I adored it as it was near the spot where we shared our first kiss, which was now a spot for bad things happening, the marina. I stepped out of my vehicle and took a great big whiff of the saltiness that was in the air. It smelled good, but it also smelled like rain and as I looked around there were clouds billowing off in the distance. I went in and made my way to the bar as Abby was already there. She looked good, she was in a skimpy little dress and her makeup was lightly done as she was showing her natural beauty as I remembered her. "Hey, you beat me here. You look gorgeous, Abby."

She gave me a warm smile. "Thank you. Yeah, it's been a long week already and I really needed a drink."

"What are you having?"

She winked at me then. "I'll get you what I'm having, if you're insisting." She gestured to the bartender for a drink for me and as we got menus and ordered, she was looked at me with those sexy peculiar eyes like she was about to ask the elephant in the room a question. "Jack, tell me what's going on at home?"

I wasn't ready for it, so I looked off in the distance. "Well, Alexis has decided to leave me. I was left with a lot of questions but now I just really don't think I care. Is that bad?"

She had a way with herself in these situations that I could remember. She gave her smirky grin while she plotted her next move. It really had me going after all these years as I never knew what she was going to do next. "Well, no it is not, Jack. This is good that this is happening."

"Oh, why is that?"

She leaned over then as our food was just placed in front of us and kissed me. It was a long passionate kiss, and she stuck her tongue deep in my mouth, so far, I could taste the tequila on her tongue. She leaned back and looked at me as she had enjoyed doing this as much as I had. "You see, now that she is out of the picture, I can swoop in for what should've been mine to start with."

"I like the sound of that, Abby. My feelings after these years have not left as I once thought." We ate and chatted a lot about what our lives had gone through. "You know, life is funny like this, it takes you on a loop and brings you back to the same person that you were truly meant to be with."

She was enjoying all that I had to say back. "I agree with you on that and I'm happy that you're not scared off I'm coming in strong."

I had butterflies then as she admitted what I thought was happening. "Abby, I would never be scared off by you or us having the ability to have a second chance. My marriage has been weird for a bit and at first, I thought it was me. Now I really don't think it is as I really don't know this person, I once thought was the love of my life. I mean not the way we are feeling after all these years." I really didn't think or worry that I technically was still married as we made each other feel good and it was genuine. We finished our food and were just about ready to pay our check. "Abby, what are you doing this evening after we're done?"

She didn't answer me at first and I was wondering what was wrong until I turned around. It was Andrea standing and listening to our conversation. "Jack, can I have a word with you?" How the fuck did she know where I was?

I excused myself from the table with Abby. "Sure." I went outside with her; she looked pissed. "What's going on? How come you're over here?"

"What in the fuck are you doing? Why does it look like you're on a date?"

"I don't owe you any answers, Andrea. Why are you over here?"

"Jack, are you on a date with this beautiful woman?"

"Maybe, but what is it to you?" I was noticing some lightning that was lighting up the sky over her just then.

"Thank you, enjoy. I'll see you soon, I'm sure and just make sure you're paying attention to me not the fucking sky!" She walked off very quickly, shaking her ass in her tight pair of leggings. But why did she follow me down here? I had put it aside as I gathered myself and went back in to see Abby.

I got back inside as there was a huge clap of thunder outside as I was hoping it wasn't awkward or the question I would expect, "Hey, sorry about that."

Then she asked that question, "Who was that weird woman?"

I could only come out with partial truth, "She's new to the town and we have had some mishaps with her workers."

Abby was smart and shooting from the hip like she always did, "Interesting, it looked like she was jealous that you were here with me."

I sat there looking at her for a moment until I said, "Oh that, nah. She wanted to ask me about what was going on at the marina."

She then called me out on my bullshit, "Jack, I've known you for a long time. I can tell when you're lying."

God damn she was good and still picked up on my little quirks. "Well, you got me. She had her way with me the other night, to be honest with you. But it was a one-time thing, and if we progress, I promise she will not get in the way of us."

She smiled at me after studying my face to see if I was telling the truth of who I was. I wanted nothing to do with Andrea on all levels, especially having sex with her. "I must go for now, Jack. I do understand, your wife left you and well everyone needs a piece of ass. I'll catch up with you, I promise."

"What, why? Abby, you never told me what you were doing this evening."

"I'm going to go to get some food and then go home. You're more than welcome to come over around 8 if you'd like."

Smiling then, I said, "I'd love that, I'll see you then."

She walked out as I ordered another drink as I sat there with a huge smile on my face, one that I hadn't had in a bit, even when Alexis wasn't around. I pounded the drink back as I checked the time and decided to get going as it was just about seven thirty. I walked out to a full-fledged thunderstorm going on and I hadn't cared if I got rained upon as I walked to my vehicle as I was impressed with the lightning that lit up the sky. I needed to go get some flowers before I went over to see Abby. She loved daisies; they were the last thing I remembered I got for her before we broke up.

When I pulled into the local market, it had just stopped raining and I was about to get out when I noticed a car that had pulled in with tinted windows behind where I was. I walked into the store to get what I was there for and upon returning, the car was gone but there was a note stuck to my front windshield.

Jack, I do apologize for our confrontation earlier. I just thought with the way things were happening so quickly for us that…. I don't know, I just thought you wouldn't think of anyone else but me. I do hope you forgive me and just think before you see this woman again. Andrea.

I must've sat in that driver's seat for a good twenty minutes as I heard some faint rumbling off in the distance. I looked up at the sky and thought better that I should go find parking over at Abby's before it pours again. I headed on over with Andrea still wedged in my mind, and the more I thought about her, the more I weirdly got excited. I sat in my vehicle for about a half hour thinking of the wild sex that she forced upon me and how much I enjoyed it. I told myself that it was a one-time thing and a fluke. She was the first woman I'd been with outside of my marriage for a long time, so of course it felt great.

I got out and walked a block to Abby's apartment. As I made it to her door, I barely even knocked, and the door squeaked open a crack. Panicked a bit, I drew my handgun and crept inside. I walked through her living room and dining room and checked her bathroom on the way by but nothing. I got up to the bedroom door which was closed as I twisted the knob and opened it slowly. I saw a blood trail from the door as I walked in and turned on the light to see the room clearer. My heart went up through my chest and almost out of my mouth. "ABBY!!!!" I screamed so hard I think the whole neighborhood heard me.

She was face down on the bed with her ass propped up in the air. There was an attempt at strangling, I could tell with her neck roughly red, but what I noticed after that had me saddened. It was one thing for her to survive the strangling but whoever was there had help as there were multiple stab wounds to her backside. She had been killed and I had a quick idea of who it was, and it then enraged me as I knew Abby would've been the one for me. Not anymore as I held her lifeless bloodied body in my arms as the sorrow surrounded me quickly again.

I held her for a few minutes as I knew what I had to do as part of the process, so I called the Gloucester police. *"Gloucester police, you're on a recorded line, what can we do for you?"*

"Yes, is Brian there? This is Chief Donaldson of the Essex police."

"Hey, Jack, sure, but can I tell him what this in regard to?"

"There's been a murder."

"Sure, one minute while I get him for you."

"Jack, what's happening?"

"Hey, Brian, I'm sorry to call you out of the blue, but I walked in and a dear friend of mine has been found murdered."

"Oh no, what's the location and I'll be there."

"311 Horse Neck Road. Don't come with the state, please."

"I'll be right over with the medical examiner."

I sat there looking at Abby and remembering the fun we had in our life. The times of passion and the times of friendship. She was always there, and I then found myself crying. "Jack, tell me what happened here?" I wasn't alone anymore as Brian was there with me now.

"Brian, yes, I was out earlier with my friend Abby Lane for some drinks when we made plans for me to come over late evening. As I was coming over, I noticed her door upon arrival opened and as I searched her apartment, I found her in bed half strangled but the stabbing is what did it."

"Do you have any idea if there was anyone that would want to harm her?"

"Well, not in her life, but there is someone that is staying in Essex I may ask."

"Jack, you know you can't do anything about this, especially if you're the only suspect."

"Suspect? Go fuck yourself, Brian!" I stormed out with rage. Of all people, he should know this wasn't my doing. He stood in the doorway looking at me. "I would never, you know I lost my wife and Abby was taking me back after all these years!" I got in my vehicle and raced away as I drove for what seemed like a lifetime, but it was only fifteen minutes to get myself back to Essex. I found myself after a blackout rage at Andrea's motel. Her men suddenly came out of nowhere as I got up to her door.

"That will be far enough, Mr. Donaldson!"

I then screamed, "Who the fuck are you to tell me anything!" I kicked one of them in the nuts as he keeled over, and I took out my handgun and pointed it at The Crusher. "Don't you fucking stop me, you big fucking idiot! ANDREA!!!!! LET ME IN NOW!!!!"

She opened the door immediately as she looked at the guy on the ground and the panic on The Crusher's face. "Come in, Jack." She bum-rushed me after I shut the door; she kissed my neck and was about to slide her hand down my pants, but I pushed her off.

I pushed her away, "Don't do this to me!"

"Jack, you know you want to do this, and if you fight it, it will only be rougher." She punched me in the gut as I fell into the bed hunched over, she took my belt off and tried tying my hands up as I kicked her away from me. I got up and as I pointed my gun at her, she only then sat there still looking at me.

She screamed then, "OWE!!!! WHAT IN THE FUCK ARE YOU THINKING AND DOING!?"

Breathing hard I screamed my question towards her cowering body, "Now that I've got your fucking attention finally! What in the fuck, Andrea! Why did you think this would be ok right now?"

She looked confused not knowing where this is all coming from, "What?"

"You goddamn know what! Trying to fuck my brains out when I was not mentally here for that!"

Still looking and acting like she thought I was there for her, she said, "Well, I didn't see you complaining when I started to kiss you. Tell me why you are the fuck here?"

I then couldn't hold it back anymore, "I fucking know what you did to Abby!"

She was calm but a confused look crossed her face. "Who the fuck are you talking about?"

"The woman you barged in on while we were having lunch today!" I pointed and clicked the gun as I was ready to fire it.

She smiled now as she responded with a question, "Oh her, what are you talking about?"

I screamed as the biggest pet peeve was being answered with a question, "I found her murdered just a short while ago!"

She looked at me, distraught, as she came closer to my face. "Then I would suggest that not happen again, you hear me? I told you don't cross me as I will bring misery to you and this fucking piece of shit town you call fuckin home!"

I didn't know what to do or say as she admitted to her murder. "Why did you do this to her?"

"Jack, whether you like it or not, you can't do this to me! Plus, I never said I did anything to her!"

I then looked at her with disgust on my face, "FUCK!!!!!"

I stormed out then and headed home as I was in no mood for anything else today. When I pulled in, I was greatly surprised to see Alexis was there but not knowing why, I automatically thought she wanted to come back. I was surprised I didn't have butterflies in my stomach as I once had for her and with the loss of Abby and the shit storm I was taking now with Andrea, I really felt sickly angered she was there. I headed into the house when I saw her chatting with a guy and as he turned around, it was the doctor from the emergency room. "Jack, you remember the doctor that took great care of you. His name is Dan and he's here to help get the rest of my things to move."

Red in the face, I punched him in the gut first and came with an uppercut that instantly broke his nose. He was on the floor, blood everywhere now as he was screaming in pain. "That's what you get for taking my wife away from me."

He got to his feet and sprayed me with pepper spray. Like that, I was down and felt him kick me not once but repeatedly. "Jack, you're a piece of shit husband that doesn't deserve a girl like me anymore. Don't ever contact me again!" Like that, there was silence as my ribs were in pain and she and Dan left. I finally started to get my eyesight when I heard a voice come from the back door.

"Jack, it's Marylin. I'm coming in."

She opened the door and found me on the ground. "Don't come in, I don't want you seeing me like this."

She never listened to me, never, and now wasn't different. "Jack, what in god sakes happened?"

Sore, I was glad that she didn't listen to me then. "Alexis was here with her doctor boyfriend and there was an altercation."

"I'm going to radio this in for his arrest!"

"Marylin, you can't!"

She was confused as she looked at me weirdly. "What, why?"

Embarrassed by the situation, I gave her my honesty. "Because I may have been the one who started it!"

She was laughing a bit now. "Jack, what were you thinking?"

I admitted more to her, "Stupidly I was thinking she changed her mind on us!"

She then came over as she looked me in the eyes and was honest, "Jack, I didn't want to tell you this, but she is not coming back. Come here." Right then and there, she lifted me up so that my back was against the lower cabinet. "Do you need to be seen?"

I was stubborn and even while I was injured, I said, "No, I'm sore, but I'll be ok."

She cleaned up my cut under my eye and as she finished, I looked at her sexy sweet face. She leaned in closer to mine and rested her forehead on mine while looking in my eyes. She then leaned her beautiful red lips into mine as we shared a kiss that seemed to last forever until she leaned back, and we both shared a quiet moment. That lasted a few minutes, "Jack, can you tell me what happened down in Gloucester today?"

Shocked by what just happened I tried to keep it hidden but I honestly answered her, "I saw an old high school friend and I was going to go over her house for some dinner when I found her strangled and stabbed multiple times!"

Mouth wide open as she held my hand, she responded, "That's horrible to hear, Jack."

"The worst part of it is, I could've seen myself with her in the future! This one hurts." I then realized what I admitted and to whom. The woman that has been throwing subtle hints at me since day one that we worked together. "I'm sorry, Marylin."

Whether it was that she knew that she still had a shot or didn't want me to know it hurt, she shrugged it off. "Jack, it's fine. No need to be sorry." Suddenly, the silence was broken with the radio that was sparked loud, *"Marylin, can you get ahold of Jack and come down to the station, please? You're going to want to see this."*

She knew how to take charge and I remembered then and there why I picked her to be my deputy. *"I'll be down as soon as I get ahold of him."*

She then slowly helped me to my feet as I turned to face out the window overlooking the back fields. She came behind me and wrapped her arms around from the backside of me, and for the first time, I felt her warmth as she held on tight. I had all the anger and sorrow let out of me, something that hadn't happened since Alexis and I were dating. It felt right. "Thank you for that, Marylin."

She smiled hearing that. "We should get going to the station, Jack."

"Agreed, I'll meet you down there."

I was at the door to the Bronco ready to leave when I was pushed awkwardly forward. I stabilized myself as I hopped into the driver's seat and shut the door. I looked out the window and saw it was The Crusher now in my headlights and he stared at me until I felt awkward. "Can I help you, Crusher?"

He barked at me then a threat I hadn't taken to heart, "Soon, you will find out why they refer to me as The Crusher!"

"Whatever, big guy! I've got more important things to tend to, so go take your muscle-bound ass back to Andrea or else!" I provoked the guy who had been trying to kick my ass from the start. He came walking over to the window and reached for my shirt to try to yank me from the vehicle. I was struggling with him now choking me, so I reached under my seat and pulled out my crowbar. I swung around and over the top of his wrists as hard as I could, hearing bones popping, but he then released his grip. I got out of the vehicle, cowering in pain, but something came over me then. I kicked him in the face with my steel-toed police boots. He fell on his back now, out cold and bloodied on the wet ground in the dark. I looked at his sorry ass face. "Don't you ever try coming to me let alone my home and think you'll have your way with me. You will never win at that war; I will always have you knocked the fuck out!" I stepped on the gas and sped off with him lying on the ground.

I ignored this as I was almost at the station, knowing he was a criminal, and he wasn't about to go to any law enforcement to press charges, but I would have to watch my back from now on. Upon my arrival, Marylin greeted me out front.

Marylin greeted me, worried, "Jack, I was going to start back over there when you hadn't shown immediately. I thought something was drastically wrong. Everything ok?"

"Yeah, Marylin, but I took out Andrea's man. The Crusher!" I hadn't given her time to react as we walked inside and when I did, there was a huge odor emanating around the office. "What in the heck is that smell? "They opened a box to show me and what I saw was gut wrenching. It was someone's hand. Someone had chopped a hand off and sent it to our office. "What is this? Where did this come from? Can I see the address label?" I went looking for the address label, but there was none. My first thought was Andrea trying to send me another warning. But this one was hardcore, even worse than she could do. "Did we get prints yet?"

Marylin squinted when she told me this. "The prints come back to an Abby out of Gloucester."

I screamed as I was in shock. "WHAT THE FUCK IS GOING ON!" Suddenly we heard a car door outside and then the front door to the station open. It was her!

Chapter 7

"Andrea, what can we help you with?"

"Can I talk to you in your office, please!" We walked into the office and soon after the door shut, she was up in my face. "Do you really want to die now, Jack? Because you really hurt one of my men tonight and I'd love to know why?"

"First off, you don't come in here making threats to the chief of police! Second, you should ask him why in the fuck was he trying to choke me!"

She didn't want any of my explanation as she slapped me in the face right then which caught me off guard. "First of all, like I said killing an innocent woman is not my thing, and as much as I'm attracted to you, that's not my style. Maybe you should look closer, and you may find that person. Don't fuck me over anymore, Jack!"

"Wait, what do you mean? You were telling me the truth about Abby!" She didn't hang around though to answer anymore. What she said threw chills down my spine. There was someone else that had strangled and stabbed poor Abby, but who?

Marylin had come in after watching this unfold. "Hey, Jack, what was that all about? Are you ok?"

"Hey, Marylin. Andrea was all in a tizzy because I beat her guy silly. Yes, I'm fine, it's not like I haven't been slapped in the face before. I mean, it's been a while."

She had sympathy on her face. "I'm sorry you had to go through that. How are you doing otherwise? I mean, I did hear about your old high school girlfriend."

For a minute I gasped to find my thoughts. "Wait, how did you find out?"

She had a grin on her face then. "I have my ways and word around here travels quick."

I tried to read her to see if she gave anything up, but it was virtually impossible. "Well, I just found out the person I thought was behind it is not. I'm upset as you know Abby was my long-lost sweetheart, I just realized I let go and now she's gone! We must investigate to find out who did this."

She put up her hands to tell me to slow down. "Jack, we cannot possibly investigate. Gloucester is not our jurisdiction. You're better off leaving it for them to figure out. You know they will." She was right, as much as I didn't want to admit it. I hung my head in my hands at my desk.

She came over behind me and started to rub my shoulders. It felt good, but I looked up as I thought people would be watching. She had closed the office shades, and she moved in closer to my ear to whisper, *"Jack, you know what you should do, you should come over to my house after work later tonight for a few drinks and relax. Come have some fun."* She gave me a small sensual kiss on the back of my neck as she then walked out knowing my answer after that. *Why would she do this at a somber time for me? She had no fucking shame.*

I got up and left as I went for a drive down to Good Harbor Beach to watch the waves. I thought about what Andrea had said about looking closer for who would've done this. I thought about the hooded killer that was still out there. Could this have been the killer's work? Suddenly, there was a tap on my shoulder. As startled as I was, I calmed down when I saw it was my friend Sam Travers. Sam and I went way back to our police academy days when we bunked together; those were the days. We used to tear up the scene when we weren't learning at school. He was essentially the person who helped me get through the academy.

"Hey, Sam, how are you doing these days?"

He was smiling with joy in his eyes. "Not too bad, Jack. I'm trying to stay busy. How about you?"

I couldn't hide anything from him, not now, not ever. "Well, I would say I'm having a shitty week let alone month. Alexis left me for some doctor over at Ipswich Hospital. Now a hooded murderer is still on the loose as well as an ex-girlfriend from high school that I was thinking about seeing again was murdered."

Assuring me it'll be fine with a hand on my shoulder then, he said, "That's a rough time, Jack. Is there anything I can do for you?"

"There's something you can do to start; can you go over and check on my wife? I know it sounds weird, but I want to make sure all is good."

He looked at me then, confused. "Yeah, is that all? I was hoping I could help you uncover who murdered your ex."

I was getting up when he said this as I stopped in my tracks to look back at him, "I'll be in touch about that part. Just be ready to assist." I never looked back. I went back to the truck and went home to get myself ready to see Marylin at her place. I didn't want to over dress, so I dressed down with a tee that showed off my toned muscles and topped it with sweatpants. I figured why get dressed if we both had sex on the mind. I found myself on her doorstep a little before six and before I could knock, she opened the door, which startled me.

"Hello, Jack, I'm glad you came over. Come on in, please."

As I got into her house, I realized this was the first time I'd ever been inside her house after ten years of working with her. "You have a nice home, Marylin." There were hunting knives out and about with rifles locked away in a glass case. I noticed in her dining room there were deer antlers and heads lined up on the wall. "I had no idea you're an avid hunter. Very impressive."

Smiling as I showed interest in her hunting, she answered, "Yes, I have been all my life. All those vacations I take, gets me away in the mountains."

"I learned something new about my deputy."

She was then smiling at me now, "You can learn a lot more from me after dinner. But for now, let's sit. I hope you don't mind I made us some steak tips and fries."

"That's perfect. Thank you. So, tell me, though, how long have you been collecting all those fancy knives?"

She was briefly super ecstatic in her answer then. "Oh, all those. You like them? I've been buying them for a good fifteen years now. They are mostly for show, unless I need them when I go fishing. Enough about me for right now. Have you heard from your wife lately?"

"Nah, I figure she will come out of the woodwork when she is ready to face us in separation."

"Well, if you need me anymore to watch her or even to see what she may be up to, just let me know."

She smiled in anticipation that I would say yes but that never came out.

"I will, thank you. I do have to say these tips are delicious." I never wanted her to know that I put Sam on that, so I knew I was equally as good at changing the subject when I wanted to.

She had her own way in changing the subject when she wanted to as she had done so now, "Thanks, I got them from one of my hunting trips last November. I'm so glad you like venison. Hey, what are you going to do about Andrea if she never leaves Essex?"

I then looked up at her at that moment. I thought it was a very random question to be asking, but her face didn't show any suspicious signs for digging for some info. "Well, I haven't given it much thought considering there's other stuff happening right now. I mean, we have the hooded murderer still out there as well as Abby's killer."

She had stopped eating for a second and glared up at me as if to see if I was serious. "Jack, I thought you were going to allow Gloucester to do their thing with this?"

"Yeah, but it doesn't mean I can't do any searching in our town."

She was very serious right then and I couldn't tell if she was nervous or just distracted as I didn't listen to her suggestion earlier, "I see. Do you have any clues?"

She kept on eating with her head in her plate as I looked up at her and noticed in a separate room beyond the dining room—what appeared to be her coat room—were a few dirty black hooded sweatshirts hanging. "No clues yet. It has only been a few days. I mean, I had thought Andrea had done this, but she honestly answered while fighting that she had no ties to this."

She then reached out and held my hand, "I will be here if you need any of my help."

We were finished eating at that point. When I looked up, she was smiling and staring at me at that moment. "Thank you, that is great to know that you have my back when I need you." She came over suddenly and bent over to kiss me. I saw she had no bra on under her tank top as her nipples were hard and now staring me in the face like a few thumbtacks. She was a very passionate kisser as our tongues locked solidly, but before she could go any further, I pushed her away and stood up. "Excuse me, Marylin, as much as you just got my motor running and you kissing me just gave my cock the best hard on, I've had in my life, I have something I've got to go tend to." I got up and left, walking a bit awkward until my cock calmed the fuck down before she could even ask what it may have been. I drove down the street and thought of going to see Andrea when suddenly the station radioed me.

It was a voice that I hadn't been expecting, *"Jack, if you are there there's a Sam wanting to speak with you, I need to patch you through to."*

"Go ahead, Sam."

"Jack, I wanted to tell you that everything has been on the norm with your wife. Do you feel like I'm still needed?"

I wanted to then check in with him as it sounded like something was off with him, *"Yes, please at least another week. Sam, is there anything bothering you right now?"*

He was hesitant for the first time ever but then started talking, *"Ok, I will stay on watching your wife. Jack, I was wondering if you made any progress finding Tom's friend?"*

Fuck, I totally forgot to check back in with him with what I found out. *"Wait, what did you say Sam? Well, that makes sense Tom hasn't bothered me about that. I'm so sorry for not getting back to him and if I knew you were helping him, I'd have gotten back sooner. This was tough but I had done all my searching and due diligence with this. What I found is that he went down to Texas. I tracked him down and gave him a call. He was hesitant to give me information at first. I explained that Tom was worried, and he couldn't have been more apologetic."*

"So, did he say what happened?"

I was hoping he didn't give me that awkward question, *"Sam, he told me he didn't want to be fishing around the area with the likely chances of a serial murderer around. He seriously wanted to be safer in his outdoors experience."*

"Thank you, Jack. I really needed to get this information. I will make sure Tom gets this, so he gets assurance of what happened." Silence followed as he left satisfied with our conversation.

I went down to the motel and knocked on Andrea's door until she finally answered. "Jack, what a pleasant surprise. You can come in." I stepped in and she was inches away from my face before she asked the question she was dying to ask. "What brings you by at this hour?"

"I was hoping I could ask you a few questions. Oh, I'm sorry if I stepped in so late."

She had a definite sexiness to her. "Jack, no need to be sorry. What can I help you with? I knew you were coming; I knew where you were." She then had my hand in hers.

I was dumbfounded right then which distracted me with my first thought. "Wait, how did you know I would be coming over?"

She smiled as she looked at me, "I knew you were over your deputy's home. I know she is not well how do I say it, alluring as I am, so I knew you'd be over for me to help. Oh, look at that stiff…"

I stopped her before she could distract me even more as I moved her hand away from my cock, "I was hoping you could reiterate what you meant earlier that I should look closer to me in that murder."

She was getting distracted with her hormones now. "I promised I would help you out. My theory is split in two. First is the hooded murderer has possibly killed your friend and the one I'm leaning towards is someone close to you may be involved."

"That's great, thank you. Can I ask you, what or who do you mean when you say someone close to me?" I went and sat on her bed for a few minutes as I contemplated things but mainly to lure her over to me. She came over immediately as a cat would for cat nip. Before I knew it, she had a lip lock on me as I pushed her off a bit. "Can you answer that question please! If you can't we can't be doing this right now!"

"Why are you doing this? Why do you care so much for this fucking small town? If you really want to know if I thought of the person who may have done this close to you, I haven't had a clue but it's just a feeling in my stomach." I looked at her and all her beauty and the longer I sat and stared, the longer she knew she had me as I was convinced, she was giving me her truth. She slowly came in and kissed me as my mind slowly drifted away from the day I had just had. She knew exactly what to do to help me relax as she slowly made love to me. Her passion was like nothing I had experienced as her moves were like any other, I've been with, hitting the intimate connection that I was trying not to go to. Our bodies were one sweating as we lay there naked afterwards, staring at the ceiling, she asked, "Jack, what are you thinking about now?"

"It's hard to explain. I mean, you have me totally relaxed now, thank you, but I guess it's about my thoughts on all that has gone down."

Her hand on my chest, she said, "Tell me. I think you should get it out as I think it would help."

My police radio startled the both of us, *"Jack, you must get down to the marina. There are a bunch of people holding some men hostage until you get there. They say they watched them take drugs off a boat."*

"Shit, I'll be right down there." I watched Andrea for any type of movement, and she was frozen. "Did you set this up so you can get your guys to move your shit into our town?"

Her mouth open as she started to give me her quick answer, "Well, how else is a girl supposed to make a business?"

"Don't fuck with me, I can easily arrest you for doing this!"

She had her way with working me over. "Oh, but you will not. Do you remember the body I helped you dispose of out of state? Yeah, that's right, you will allow me to get my pills into this town or else!" I was still on my tracks now as she came out with what I had almost pushed out of my mind. "Besides, I feel a connection between us as I know you do. We have had some great sex not to mention I love the way you feel inside me."

I gave her a kiss on her forehead as I left her without a word and drove down to the marina. There was a mob around six of her guys, and they weren't happy. "Alright, you all can disperse and go home." They all left quickly, but one of the guys tried telling them off as he was laughing. I slammed him on the ground. "What the fuck is so funny? You're under arrest!"

"For what?"

"Distribution of drugs through my beloved town! Stand up, NOW!" I cuffed each one of those pricks and it felt good. I got ready to head back as backup came to clean the mess left behind. Then a radio message came through that I would never forget, *"Jack, you may want to go over to check on your friend Sam."*

"Yeah, well I'm busy with some people I just arrested."

Then it sounded urgent, *"You may want to go now! His call was a distressed one!"*

I put on my siren and sped over to where Sam was at. When I pulled up on his car, some of the guys in the back were laughing, but I ignored it. I drew my gun, which felt like a lifetime since I needed it, and walked slowly over to Sam's Cadillac. As I approached it, I opened the door to see him bent over the steering wheel. I couldn't believe what had happened to him. He was strangled but fought it and stabbed multiple times in the back of the head. He lay there against the steering wheel with blood dripping all over the place. My first thoughts were poor Sam never saw it coming. I called it in to the Ipswich police and while I waited for them to come and secure the scene, I went over to go check on Alexis and the baby.

Suspiciously enough I hadn't even made it to the front door, there was a spotlight that hit. The doctor that she was seeing answered the door as if he was expecting me then. "Jack, what are you doing here?"

"Checking in on you guys. Can't I do that?"

He was cocky in his answer just then. "Don't you think if she wanted this that she would ask? Besides isn't this out of your jurisdiction?"

"Alexis! I need to see you and the baby right now!"

She was confused and sleepy at the same time. "Jack, what is this all about? We were all sleeping! See, we are both safe and fine! Now that the baby is awake, can you tell me what the fuck is going on for you to be at our house right now?"

"I can't go into a lot of explanation, but there was a murder out front of here."

"Jack, that's your fucking job again. Just go indulge into it like you always do and leave us the fuck alone." She shut the door in my face. I was boiling it over. She seemed like she was all fine and good. She didn't need me checking in on her never wanted further to contact from me.

"Go to fucking hell, the both of you!" I gave up right then and there and decided to indulge in the job like it was my best side chick to take my mind off my failed marriage.

"Jack, are you ok?" It was Marylin; she had come over in her street clothes, ripped booty showing in her shorts and a tight little tank. "I heard you yelling all the way around the corner."

"No, I'm not ok. There was a murder of one of my old friends and all I wanted to do was check in on my soon-to-be ex-wife and baby. They shut the door in my fucking face."

"Jack, there's nothing you can do here. You do realize that Ipswich police are here now taking care of everything now?" She always tried to get reasoning in me before I went off the deep end.

I was so out of it I had thought I was giving in to my own department to take care of the murder scene, but in fact it was Ipswich. "I guess I need to get away from this scene. I forgot we are in Ipswich." I looked at her and it must have been a rough look as she came in to hug me. Her perfume turned me on instantly as it was the same one that Alexis had always worn to get me going. "You smell really good, Marylin; how did you know that was my favorite perfume?"

She was alluring then. "Jack, why don't we go back to my place, and I can help you unwind?"

"I'm sorry Marylin, this is not a great time for me to come back over. I have a few uh, things to go take care of." I didn't want her to know as I knew what I needed to go do next with Andrea's guys.

She was curious as she always was. "Ok, so tell me will I see you after?"

"Marylin, have a great night."

I went back to my Bronco, and I drove off. As I got away from the scene and was in between Ipswich and Essex, one of the guys yelled from the back seat, "Hey fuck face! You can pull over up here." I looked back as he was serious about what he said and as I slowed down to a stop. I looked over into the marsh that wasn't far off and there was a boat with lights on. I got out and opened the back door as I looked at these two, he added another demand, "Take these cuffs off so we can bounce!" I unlocked the handcuffs on them both as they got out and gave me a grave look then. I had thought they would forget but they didn't, "Give us our guns now as well. Come on, we need to get going."

I gave them their handguns as one was a foot in the weeds as the other then held his gun to my throat then. "I really don't like you, asshole. You're so lucky you're fucking the boss. You will get yours soon enough." I wasn't scared of him as he slowly backed into the weeds and they both disappeared. I then hopped into the Bronco and decided to just drive and think.

Chapter 8

I had found myself back at Marylin's place, and the more I fought with myself over this decision, my evil thoughts came up with reasoning to make me go through it; I needed more information about my deputy in case she is the hooded murderer. I had to be careful because on the one hand if she was, I didn't need to put myself in harm's way, and on the other side of it, I hadn't wanted our relationship between each other to be sour. I had been avoiding this for some time now because of our working relationship. Now it seemed tempting with the fact I was going to eventually be single once again.

She couldn't hold her excitement in, "Jack, come in. I'm happy to see you took me up on my offer earlier."

"I was glad to have finished up quick with my things and yeah I was hoping that your offer was still open let alone you were still awake."

She giggled, "Jack, you're funny. You of all people should know we don't sleep right. I was going to be up for a while and yeah, I was hoping you'd be by." She came up to me and she started hugging and kissing me as she led me up to her bedroom and along the way I was trying to find out if there was anything on her walls to tip me off, but there was nothing. I was now face to face with her in her bedroom as she stripped me and pushed me onto her bed. She then dropped her shorts and ripped off her tank top. She stood there in all her beauty as I was mesmerized that my deputy was hotter than I expected. She then came over and sat on top of me as she enjoyed every moment riding me slowly and passionately kissing me. She moved her hips like the motion of a gentle wave, with each move she was getting closer to climax. We finally swapped positions to give her a break as she laid on her back and spread her legs open, I slid into her warm moist vagina. She felt great as we fucked our tension off for hours; it seemed like until we both hit climax for seemed like the fifth time. We sweated out all our issues when we were done, and I had no regrets about sleeping with her as she and the situation felt rightfully good.

I lay there for a while, staring at the ceiling. Then I turned to look over at her; she was sound asleep already. I got dressed and snuck out of the bedroom and downstairs. I tripped on a stool that I didn't remember being there and almost screamed bloody murder. Thankfully, she seemed like a sound sleeper as she never woke up from that. I went over to the place where I saw the black hooded sweatshirts, but they weren't there. Where could they have gone? I then tried what appeared to be a door to the basement, but it was locked. Who locks their door to the basement? I felt around a bit more with what I could in the dark and found nothing. I was upset I didn't get that chance to check what I came over for, but I was glad to know how a great roll in the hay it was even though it may come back to bite me someday.

I started driving and thinking about Marylin and the odd things in her home that could make her a prime suspect, but nothing really tied her to the black-hooded murderer. As I pulled into my driveway, I was greeted by Andrea sitting on my porch right where Alexis had always sat. "Hello, Andrea, what can I do for you?"

She was smug right then. "Hello, Jack, I was hoping I'd catch you coming home eventually."

"Yeah, how long were you here waiting for me?"

She looked at her watch when she answered me, "Oh, it has been a while. But that's not what's important. Can I come in a talk to you?"

I did what I needed to do now as I looked at her as exhausted as I was. "Sure, come on in." I got out some Jack Daniels as it was a long day and gave her a glass as she would never refuse one. "So, what do you want to chat with me about?"

"I know what happened tonight and where you went immediately afterwards." She reluctantly stared at me, waiting for my response.

"Yeah, so what's it to you? You got what you wanted with your men being freed." I gave her what I usually do when I wanted to get a point across.

"Well, please don't be fresh, I want to help. I know why you went to your deputy's, and I know it wasn't to just have sex."

"Well, you're right on that even though it did feel right but I know it was so wrong. But it felt good to have had my cock buried inside her."

Snooping was in her business, and she was intrigued. "It felt right?" She came up to my face and asked, "You really enjoyed the feel of her pussy?"

"Andrea, yes, it's been a while that I've had sex and yes so what I enjoyed her pussy, so fucking what! Now you mentioned how you can help me.

She smirked at me as she drank the glass of whiskey slowly. "Well, I can say that you probably found nothing that ties her to the murders that have been going around, and you don't want to find anything as she is a really great deputy, right? Let alone her juices taste good and feel even better wrapped around that hard..."

I didn't let her finish then, "Yeah, your point?"

"I think you should look outside the box on this one and no I'm not talking sex now either. I have had one of my men out there in a few situations looking and he is getting somewhere." Right then, she put the glass down, walked over to me, and leaned down to try and kiss me, but I pulled away.

"Are you going to fill me in on anything he has seen so far?"

"I will when I find out solid information." She sat on my lap facing me as she put down my glass and started to kiss me. The kissing was so intimate with her luscious lip and her soft touch that my mind had thought about since I was last with this woman. She undid my pants and revealed no underwear, and my cock as hard as can be as she then lifted her skirt up with no panties on, she had slid right down on me. She helped take care of my need now while she straddled me as she twirled her hips and all her juice all over my throbbing cock. We were both about to climax and as we did together, I felt even more relaxed and weirdly connected with this woman. This random woman I had just met, that was this scary head of an organization, had me feeling that we knew each other forever. It was a moment that felt like forever as we looked into each other's eyes and knew what we were thinking. "Wow, that was unbelievable, Jack! I should thank you wife for leaving you."

"You're not so funny. Ok, that was a bit funny. This was great, Andrea, but I'm afraid that with your criminal ties, it will not be good for us."

She was fixing herself back up to leave when she put her soft warm hand on my chest for assurance. "Jack don't think that way. We can figure that out later. Right now, I must get going to see if I can get some beauty sleep before some serious business tomorrow."

"Wait, what business? I mean, you must tell me as this is still my town."

"You're cute, Jack, but last time I checked it was our town. The business that I have is the unloading of a pill shipment that needs to go out to Gloucester."

"Andrea, I had a feeling that was you!"

"Jack, I can expect your cooperation to turn the other cheek so I can get this business done." I was silent as I didn't want to arrest her and her gorgeous body. I suddenly looked the other way as she came in to kiss my forehead. "I thank you for this. You will not regret our newfound relationship."

She left but she had a seductive way with me that I almost felt taken for in the moment, but I quickly forgot as the sex certainly felt great.

The night got away from me as it wasn't what I was planning for as I had two women in totally different situations that were making me feel better giving themselves to me after Alexis left me. I looked at the time and it was only five in the morning as I was making some coffee and turned on the radio to listen to the news. *"Breaking News. Just in, there was another murder in Gloucester overnight as police are saying the black-hooded serial killer has struck again. This time it was a couple along the boulevard as they were caught in the middle of passion. What is this person doing, may we ask?"* I thought the same thing, *why are they going after people having sex in public? I mean, it must have something to do with this person not liking this.* Suddenly the phone rang, and it caused me to fall on the floor as it startled the fuck out of me.

"Hello, this is Jack."

"Jack, it's Andrea. I need you to come down to the room and see me before you head to the office."

I wanted her bad, but my exhaustion had the better of me then. "I will do this, but please no sex right now. I have a feeling it's going to be a busy day."

"That's fine, I have no time for that anyway, love. Now get your ass down here."

The thoughts quickly changed and left my reality. As I was taking the five-minute drive, I wondered what it might be that was so urgent. I was also thinking of the passion I had as it felt wrong, it also felt right with both women. I suddenly snapped out of it as I found that I had arrived, and she was outside to greet me. "Andrea, what's going on right now?"

"Two things, handsome. One is, there is an issue down at the docks for my business to go smooth."

Confused I asked her, "What is the issue?"

"Your deputy is down there patrolling the place. My guys have been waiting to dock now for about an hour." She was angry but sexy at the same time. She wanted to get her point across, and she did, but she made herself want to be taken.

I paused a minute to catch my thoughts. "Fuck! What do you suppose I do with this?"

"I don't give a fuck what you do, just make her go away!" She was stoned face after this, and I'd never seen her this way. I knew she needed this done.

"Uh, I will do what I can to make that happen. What is the second?"

"Jack, you know that doctor your soon-to-be ex-wife has hooked up with?"

"Yes, what is going on with that?"

"He is not who you think he is." She pissed me off a bit as she was as bland as can be with me.

"You're going to have to give me more info than that!"

"Jack, I've confirmed he's the biggest drug trafficker in the northeast. He's dangerous and he has no respect for any woman or relationship."

"Andrea, come on! Really? How long have you've known this for?"

"It's not what you think. I have known of him for many years when I've conducted business out west and only heard stories of him. I've never met him and always thought he conducted his business as a ghost. But I always thought he was living in a Boston or New York and not this small town."

"I've got to go." I knew the station was the last on my list as I rushed to leave.

"Jack, please, the docks before anything else!"

"Yes, you have my word I will get her out of your way."

Chapter 9

I was restless with my thoughts of what I was about to do, and the fight in my inner self about the whole situation was bothersome. I knew what decision I had to make, but it seemed tough and as I drove down Conomo Point towards the docks, I noticed it was quiet as I circled around to check out the area first until I saw Andrea's car pull in. Oh, I had to go quickly to try to intercept her as I parked next to Marylin's car and as I got out, I heard the boat out in the water, and it sounded like it was just offshore waiting. I didn't see

Andrea or Marylin around which made me think how quickly Andrea move. I walked down to the pier first to see if she was there, but it was empty. I looked off in the distance in the water and saw Andrea's men just waiting word, but suddenly I heard a crack in the woods behind me. I went over to see if it was Marylin and as I made my way closer, **Swoosh,** a turkey came lunging out towards me and scared the living shit right out of me. FUCK! I hated being jumpy, especially when it feels raw down here as I turned around and headed back to the water's edge slowing down at Marilyn's car and as I peeked inside, I saw she had left her radio behind.

"AHHHHHHH!"

"Who's there? Where is that scream coming from? I'm coming to help!" I ran over to a brush patch and what I saw was disturbing. It was Andrea, she was face down and hemorrhaging from multiple stab wounds to her back. I leaned down to see if she still had a pulse, but she was quickly gone.

"Jack!"

"Marylin, I'm over here in the brush."

Marylin was suddenly there, and she was nervously shaking. "I heard the scream down on the other side of the dock and I came running as soon as I could. Oh no!"

"Yeah, it looks like the hooded murderer struck again. But how could I miss any clues that this person was here? I mean, what did this person have with Andrea? I mean, I know she wasn't exactly the nicest person but still." I was even more angry now as I looked at her, so much life and such a great lover and now gone like Abby!

"I'm sorry, Jack. I will go call this in."

As I remained looking down at her bloodied body, I suddenly thought that with the unfortunate death of Andrea, maybe perhaps we could stop the drugs once and for all from coming ashore. "Wait, Marylin. Before you do that, I have an idea. It looks like when I pulled in that she had her guys in the bay waiting for something. I can flag them to come in."

"When they do, we can bust them! I love the way you think. Yes, let's do this."

"Excellent, can you give me a second with the dead body." She walked away and as I looked at Andrea, I started to feel a sadness of what could've been. "Andrea, I'm so very sorry this had happened to you. I promise I will arrest this person who did this to you." I brushed myself off and stepped out as Marylin was waiting. "Alright, I think you should pretend that you're driving away. You know where that little semi open cove is on the hill?"

Her excited self went for her vehicle immediately, "Yes, you want me to park there. That's genius as I could see everything that's happening."

"Yes, that's the plan. So, when you see them start unloading, that's when you call for backup and come down to assist in the arrest."

She then got into her car and as she looked at me with a huge smile, I noticed she was way too chipper for yet another murder that happened here in town. Maybe it was nothing, but it bothered me to see her looking like this. I just could not focus on that right now. I waved Andrea's men ashore and geared myself up for what needed to be done. They got closer and closer until they finally docked. There were three of them that were on board and all of them seemed cautious before they shut the boat's engine off. "The coast is finally clear. My apologies about my deputy. She tends to be a tad bit nosy sometimes, specifically when she thinks something may be getting ready to happen."

"Is she finally fucking gone? I mean, it delayed everything for over an hour. Andrea will be pissed if we don't get moving!"

"I'm sorry, I don't believe I've met you guys before."

They were almost screaming at me then, "What does it matter?"

"I know almost every one of her men, that's why."

They acted cocky and smug with their answer, "We are the trio that gets this shit done! That's all you need to know for now."

"Ok, fine with me. I'll let you boys get to your business."

"Wait, where do you think you're going, you, cocky mother fucking piece of shit they call the chief?"

"I must go back to work. Why?"

"You're not going anywhere until our truck gets here and we load it. You're going to be our lookout." They all looked at each other now as they were trying to understand why I wasn't fight this.

This was what I was hoping for, but I had a bad feeling that they didn't trust me. "Ok, whatever. I mean that wasn't part of what Andrea and I had agreed to."

Suddenly, he was face to face with me and I felt sick to my stomach, as if something bad was about to happen. "I know who you are to Andrea; I really don't like or agree with what she is doing with you." He went on board the boat and as their truck was backing in, I swore he mumbled about Andrea attracted to cock that she really shouldn't be enjoying. I watched as they were unloading what appeared to be a small pallet, maybe about twenty bricks of cocaine, off the boat first and into the back of the truck. Then another guy was carrying another huge amount of marijuana.

"How much more do you guys have to unload? I can't guarantee people will not be nosy soon."

"We're about to unload the last of it." Just then, all three of them were pulling off a huge number of pills in what appeared to be baggies.

Being the prying person I was, I asked the only obvious question, "What the fuck is that?"

"This is what will make us as well off as you rich people. Half the load is speed, and the other half is for people to make meth." They continued to move the product at a brisk pace when I heard Marylin starting to drive down. "Well, this is the last bit of it." He was shutting the door when suddenly Marylin pulled around the corner with her sirens on and back up right behind her.

"FREEZE!"

The last guy was stumbling to get his footing as he tried to lunge into the truck when I grabbed and threw him to the ground. "You're not going anywhere."

Suddenly I heard something behind me, **CLICK**. "I would suggest you let him go so we can go on our way!"

I held my place for a minute as I felt him lower his gun closer towards me even more. **BOOM!** *Where did that sound come from?* "You shot my guy? Andrea will make you pay for this!"

Suddenly, Marylin and other police came over as the guy she apparently shot fell out of the truck next to me with a single gunshot wound to the head. I wasn't paying attention to all of what was happening; the guy I had on the ground had maneuvered himself out of the hold I had on him and now was standing.

"You are not so tough now that I'm standing." He then pulled out a gun and pointed it at me. "You will pay for all of this, you asshole!" **BOOM!** Suddenly there was blood splattered and brain fragments all over my uniform as the guy fell to the ground. I then realized Marylin came through again for me when I reached for my own gun and realized that guy had stolen it.

She came rushing over to me then. "Jack, are you ok?"

"Yes, I'm fine. Thank you for that. I guess I was lucky you were here to save my ass." I heard kicking and screaming right then when it went to blood curdling gagging. I rushed around the other side as I saw one of the officers I'd never seen before walk away from him. The third guy was on the ground as I felt his pulse; he was dead. I looked up to find that officer, but he was gone. "Marylin, where did that officer go? What was his name? I don't remember meeting him before."

She had all the answers for me as I still wasn't sure who that person was. "Jack, calm down. I don't know what you're talking about! He had lunged at me and there was a bit of a scuffle and as I was about to get my ass kicked, he then came out of nowhere as I tried to kick him off me. There was a struggle as he was a fighter and I had to choke him off until he went limp. That's when I heard your scuffling and came to your rescue."

I didn't know what to think as I looked at the dead body and then back at her as she was starting to rub my back. "I'm so confused on all of this. I guess I should be happy we cleaned this mess up. I have to say right now you're going to clean this mess though." Just then, the state police arrived.

She was my deputy for a reason and if I did have doubt there was none now. "I promise, I will make statements and clean this mess up."

"Thanks, I must get away from here right now for a bit. I'll see you back at the station."

I was enroute to the station when I noticed I was being followed by a truck I hadn't seen around for a bit. I pulled into the parking lot of one of my favorite restaurants, The Skipper's Galley, and the truck pulled in next to me. The window rolled down and it was Frank. "Hello there, Jack, I was getting ready to head out of town, but I couldn't get a hold of Andrea. Can you let her know that I'll be back in the winter at some point."

"Frank, I will let her know when I do see her. I haven't seen her since last night."

"Ha, I know you'll see her around." He grinned after he said that to me.

"What the fuck does that mean?"

"It means she has her way with you as well as all of us. She does really like you though and you're welcome on taking care of that last guy back there on the scene. See you in the winter. Have fun fucking her brains out."

"Wait, before you go, that was you that shot the last guy dead?"

He was driving off as he was yelling one last thing that I would never repeat, "You really think we would let any of those guys get arrested and talk? Be safe, Jack." I gathered myself as I shrugged it off as I didn't want anyone to know of my relations with Andrea. I mean now it was all done as she was dead at the hands of a serial killer out there. A serial killer I must get back to work to find. I got back to the station, and it was all business and quiet as I sat in my office, I realized my head was starting to spin and getting nowhere in thoughts of where to begin on this fucking serial killer.

"Jack, it's Marylin."

It had been a few hours when she finally got in touch with me. *"Hey, how is it going down there?"*

"It's just about wrapped up. The state police are cleaning up; the coroner's office has just left. I will be back there soon. Oh, and Andrea's body couldn't be found at the scene."

"WHAT! How is that even possible?"

"Jack, I'm on my way back. We can chat when I'm back."

"Sounds like a plan, thank you for the update."

My thoughts of Marylin saving my life, being there at the right time, made me warm at first. What if she hadn't been there? I thought it was weird at first that she was the only person on the scene when I realized Andrea was murdered. But after she saved my ass, I knew she had nothing to do with it. Being thankful I was alive after all that went down, I felt the need to go visit Alexis and try to get to see my kid.

I had arrived where she was staying with the doctor when he greeted me at the door. It wasn't far off from her sister as Sam had told me after a few nights of surveying as he answered the door, "What can I do for you, Jack?"

"Oh well first, let's see, if you're going to be fucking my wife, I should know your name. Seeing it's only fair you know mine!"

He went to shake my hand and on his forearm was a tattoo I read quickly that said, Marine Corp, 1976-1982. "Sure, my name is Fred. It is a pleasure we can formally meet. Now what can I do for you?"

"Listen, I didn't come over to create issues. I had a rough day, and I was wondering if I could see my wife and child, please."

He looked at me and my facial expression. "Sure, it looks like you had one of those days."

"Yes, so very lucky to be alive."

He closed the door behind him. "ALEXIS!"

"Fuck, what does he want!"

Fred had spoken in a loud calming demeanor just then, "I think you should oblige; he's not here to start." She didn't sound happy that I was here again, but after a few moments, she appeared with the baby in her arms.

"Jack, I wasn't expecting you. Is everything ok?" she asked, looking like she had just rolled out of bed and was pissed off she had to see me.

The baby warmed up to a smile and wanted to be in my arms. I held her for the first time in a while and I forgot all about my day already. "Yes, it is now. It has been a very rough day, and I'm thankful to be alive and enjoying this moment."

Just then she changed her attitude, "Talk to me, tell me about it."

I handed the baby to her as I got my fill, and I kissed the baby on the cheek and held Alexis's hand briefly. "It has come to my attention that Fred is one of the largest drug dealers around. Did you know that?"

She didn't look at me at first as I knew that was a yes, "What the fuck are you in our business for? Jack, we are not together and if this is what you came over for then..."

Smiling nervously, I looked at her, "Thank you, I will be in touch. I can't talk about it now. Just please be open to coffee soon." I walked away as she was watching me. I really didn't want to bring up the day I had as I got an awful feeling when I was there. Fred seemed like a nice guy, but I truly didn't need Alexis to confirm with her words of who he is.

"Yes, I will come in when I have a chance." I left her watching me drive away; she looked concerned like she used to when I had a rough day. I really wasn't sure if the concern was for me or what I knew but either way time would tell. I got back to the station, and as I was walking in, Marylin pulled in right after. *I thought she would've been here by now.*

"Hey, I'm back now, Jack. I'm going to go get that paperwork done, but first can I talk to you in your office." I motioned for her to go ahead first as she turned on the light and I shut the door. She didn't waste any time. "Do you think she framed herself dead so we could not be on her anymore?"

"I really don't think so. I mean, Marylin, she didn't have much reason to do so."

She looked perplexed at me for a few moments, "I mean I really don't think you'd help her do any illegal activity. It's just weird."

I watched her as she left my office and sat down at her desk to start the paperwork on the dealings that just happened. She was diligently working and when I wasn't looking at her, when I did look back up, she was staring me down. It was a death stare that gave me the chills. *But why, I mean besides sleeping with her and having some great passion, I don't believe I gave her the wrong idea. Could she suspect that Andrea was a major drug player, but better yet does she know I had sexual relations with her.*

Chapter 10

I was working out in the new gym we had put in behind the station. It was a place where I could do my deep thinking when I needed some quiet time. I was fifteen minutes into my workout as I was thinking how suspicious Marylin has been lately. I couldn't quite make anything out on her to make any suspicions reality yet. Is she really that good to be on to me? "Jack?" Suddenly after the door opened, I heard Marylin call my name. It was not unusual for her to come and find me, and as she rounded the corner when I was in a mid-leg press, she had a perplexed smile on her face. "Hey, I thought I'd find you here when I didn't see you in your office."

"Yeah, I needed some alone time to think."

"Would I be a bother if I joined you?" She was hoping to as I could see it in her face.

"No, not at all. You can spot me on the bench, if you don't mind."

We moved over to the bench press as I set the weight to 200 pounds and lay down. She got over me as she guided me and watched as I lifted. "Jack, do you have any ideas on solving this murder spree?"

I almost dropped the weight back down on me as I wasn't expecting her to come right at it with things. She helped me get the weight back safely as I took a deep breath and sat up and looked at her now standing in front of me. "No, I don't have any ideas yet. Do you have any thoughts to share?"

"I was hoping you'd ask me. Now we have Andrea's guys at the coroner's office…"

I abruptly interrupted her then, "Uh, I wanted to tell you that they are a dead end. We would have to catch the next round if there is any."

She almost blustered the next thing out like a hot cup of coffee, "Fuck! You're right! Why did it have to happen like this?"

"Well, they really didn't want to be caught as they thought they would be dead otherwise."

She pushed the next envelope, "I still would love to know what your relationship was with her. Do you believe it was an act, you know her death?"

I smiled calmly at her. "My relationship was just a working one. When we had to mingle, we did just that. If I knew her it might be an act, or her guys already scooped her body up. We shall not know for sure unfortunately.

"Perhaps you're right. I just would hate for her to come back with a vengeance on you and this town."

"Why are you so fucking hung on this right now? I mean we have a serial killer out there and you continue to press me over something that has dissipated for now at least."

She pressed one last time, "I don't know, and don't get sore now. I guess I would love to arrest some of them and see how much we could make them squirm. I mean they brought drugs and violence to our town."

"That's not going to happen! Do you have any other thoughts?"

She looked pissed at this point, but what came out of her mouth I was not expecting. "The other thing I was going to say is that I suspect that doctor that Alexis is seeing."

"Why do you say this?"

She took a deep breath before talking then, "When you had me watching them a bit ago, I noticed sometimes he went out at night and not to work."

She lay down after setting the weight and as I helped her, I said something that will always remind me of the ghostly face that she had in mid-lift. "It is not what you think with him. Why are you so much on a witch hunt to solve this so fucking quickly? You cannot reach on fucking things we don't know yet! I mean I can tell you I found out in some digging that he is a very high drug dealer but don't read into it until I find more info out, please. I don't want to think negative, Marylin, as I feel we are getting close to solving this. I just feel things will fall into place soon." I was not paying attention as she had struggled, and the weight slipped briefly to her chest. I watched her struggle before lifting it up off her and she sat up, caught her breath, and looked up at me.

"I thought you'd be wanting to quickly solve this shit as you lost two women you were very attracted too. Oh, also what the fuck was that? You watched me struggle a minute before lifting it!"

I went back down and lay there as I thought about what she said. "I think you are jealous, or at least it sounds like that and I wanted to let you see how it feels to struggle and figure yourself out in a pinch!"

She caught on as she gave me a dirty look, "No, I'm not jealous. So, you did have something for Andrea!"

"Oh, good lord, you got me. Yes, I thought Andrea was a sexy woman, but…"

She smiled then. "Jack, calm down. Your secret is safe with me. I know that means you had more than a working relationship. I'm not no way jealous as I just wanted you to admit it. You are normal with no wife now to be you know."

"Yes, I know and thank you for understanding. Good, then if I'm being honest, I will tell you now that I'm going to try to make a play to get Alexis back." I went for the weight and lifted what I thought was 200 but now 225 and as she guided me to the spot and let go, she didn't look so happy.

"Are you fucking crazy? Jack, she left you. You can't tell me you're thinking you have a chance to get her back."

I was struggling as she was watching me with humor on her face but perhaps it was payback from moments ago of her struggle. I was giving her the look to help but she was watching me struggle as it slowly sank down inches away from my chest before she slowly guided it back up. "What the fuck was that about Marylin?"

"Jack, you need to think of what's most important to you right now. Remember you need to struggle to figure things out! I think trying to get that bitch of a wife back in your life is a bad move. I also think we could have something."

"Marylin, Marylin!" She walked out as the conversation went south immediately. Whatever she was thinking, coming to me with this wasn't the best time. There was something she was hoping for with us that wasn't quite there. I went into the shower a few minutes later to cleanup before I went back to work for the overnight when I heard shoes hit the floor. "Hello?"

"Hey, Jack, I hope you don't mind me joining you in here." Marylin had not only come back but let herself into the shower and was now naked behind me. She was massaging my shoulders a bit as I was tense. This was shocking that she would be this open with things and risk someone coming in and seeing us.

"You really shouldn't be in here with me." She then turned me around and as we faced each other; I was then silenced by her soft passionate kissing. I wanted to push her away but couldn't as she had me in trance with her beauty and her soft lips. We kissed for a what seemed like a long time and as she slowly gripped my cock and was stroking it hard, I reached for her and as I slipped a finger in her now-moist clit, she moaned in the moment. That was the sexiest moan and jump that really turned us up a notch as she turned her ass around as she guided my cock into her now wet vagina. We were good at that moment in knowing we needed to keep the noise to a minimum as she put a hand towel in her mouth to stop herself from really moaning as she was grinding into me with every thrust that I had given to her. She was just about to climax the second time and as she did, she knew I hadn't yet. So, she turned around with a very naughty look, leaned up against the wall, and slid one leg up over my shoulder. She rested her foot near my ear as I slid my cock deep inside her as we were face to face. It was the wildest sex that I'd ever had as I didn't last much longer. We climaxed and slowed down as we looked at each other and kissed as I knew I was in trouble. That sex we had in the shower that day was unbelievable as it was the wildest that I'd ever had I knew it was trouble as it may interfere with our working relationship. But I didn't care at that moment as it made me feel good. I even noticed a tattoo on her lower back while I was watching her cute ass from above. It was a sexy color but unique. It was a pair of red high heels and the red had me turned on, but it was the weirdest place for a tattoo let alone high heels. I was deep in thought when she finished and was then face to face with me.

"That was ferocious, Jack."

"Yes, it was indeed, but maybe we shouldn't have done that."

She kissed me then, perhaps to shut me up. "I didn't see you backing away or pushing me off. You're welcome." She disappeared out of the shower then and when I gathered myself and went out, she was gone. I looked around and found a note that she had left for me. A weird one to say the least.

Jack, that was some of the best sex I've had in my life. We will be together as much as you say we shouldn't. You will give in to the fact you're so very attracted to me as much as I am to you. I'm taking a few days off to do some thinking about us. When we go forward with a relationship, I promise we will figure something out. But for now, I wanted to let you know I appreciate every inch of you!

Had she gone fucking insane? This sounds like a stalkerish letter, but perhaps I never had someone that cared for me as much as she did. No, I will not be taken for here until I find out if she was for real. I knew deep down inside that I wanted to try to see if Alexis would come back to me. But I also had this weird feeling that Marylin was up to something that she wasn't supposed to be up to. She had a secret side of her life that I would somehow find out and honestly, I deeply wanted to find out.

I walked back into the station and the few that were there were staring at me and even the only other woman on the force was smiling in the corner as she left. I ignored all of that and went about my business. "Darren, can you come in here for a minute?" Darren, one of my top police officers in the department, was close with Marylin and as we all thought he has a crush on her, I figured I would press him to see if she told him anything. "Have a seat, buddy." I had just shut the door when he peered out of the side of his eyes, almost looking like he felt he was in trouble.

"Mr. Donaldson, it feels like I'm in trouble."

"Nah, Darren, you could not ever do anything wrong. Relax, I just have a few questions I'd love to ask you."

"Sure, sir, go ahead. I will answer whatever I can for you."

I just came out with it, "Are you still kind of close with Marylin?"

He was shy on answering but came out with what I thought he might, "How do you know this, sir?"

"Everyone knows that you have a crush on her, buddy. It's ok if you do."

He was relieved but curious at the same time where I was going with this, "Well yes, I do, but that's beside the point. To answer your question, I'm still close to her, why?"

"Did she tell you anything of what she might be up to the next few days while she is out on a few vacation days?"

"All she said was she had some sort of business she had to take care of to make life a bit easier for things and people. When I asked her more, she shot me a look and I know those looks mean stop pressing. She did, however, say she was going to spend it in Ipswich."

"Ipswich? What is there for her?"

The next thing he said had my thoughts racing more. "She said she had a private eye gig she needed to try and wrap up and then she was going to spend a day at Crane's Beach. She doesn't indulge over what she wants me to know and honestly, I don't think she looks at me the same way as I look at her."

I felt bad for him momentarily with his sad look, "Darren it's ok buddy, you can win over all the ladies. Thank you for this information, Darren. This was a huge help."

"No problem. If you ask me, I feel she has a fascination for someone here at work. She really needs to get laid!" Little did he know it was me that she had a fascination over, and she was getting fucked and not laid.

"Why do you say that?"

He was a bit on edge with the next thing he told me. "There have been multiple times where I have caught her masturbating in the gym. I have asked her what she was thinking, and she storms off."

"Can you show me where in the gym you caught her?"

"Sure." We walked down to the gym and as we went inside the empty place, he went right over to the corner where I was just benching. "Right here on this bench." He was looking for my response or even a facial expression, but I was silent for a few minutes. "Sir, are you ok?"

The reason I didn't say anything was I wanted to sit in the spot where Darren had pointed out to search my inner self for answers and as soon as I looked around, I didn't see anything that popped when frustration hit. Perhaps it was because she was so mysterious for so long or because I hadn't seen what was possible in front of me and either way, I looked up at the sky out the window and as I did, I caught a great view of my office. "Fucking a!" She was getting off watching me as I was in my office! This was not upsetting but getting me weirdly turned on.

"What is it, sir?" The kid was super confused and scared at the same time.

"Darren, you are dismissed from this now. I appreciate your time in answering my questions. Please keep this between you and I."

"Yes, sir. Just tell me, is she in trouble of some sort?"

"Darren, I don't think so, but if she is, I can't really disclose that to you."

Chapter 11

I paced the gym for a bit as I thought of what I was going to do to try to figure out what Marylin was up to. I didn't have anyone to rely on as my only guy who could do some spying for me got murdered. I walked back up to the station and sat in my office as I picked up the phone to make a call. *"Hello, this is Maren, please leave a message after the tone."* **BEEP.**

"Maren, it's Jack. Can you do me a huge favor and please keep an eye out down the street at 72 High Street. That's where Alexis is staying. I don't trust the guy she is with right now. Thank you." Maren is my younger sister by a few years, and she always did favors for me; we were much closer than Alexis thought we were. But Maren loved Alexis as well and would do anything to make sure she was safe. At one point, I almost thought Maren had a crush on her, but it was my thoughts running away with me. She didn't know yet that she left me, but I really didn't think that would faze her. I was well into some deep thoughts when I got startled with the phone ringing.

"Hello, this is Chief Donaldson."

"Jack, it's Maren. I just got your message. I had no idea that you two were having issues within the marriage. Are you doing, ok?"

"Yes, she left me because she didn't want me in harm's way anymore with this job. She wanted me home more often as she thought I was not paying attention to her with my hours." She had no response,

and the silence was killing me. *"Maren, are you judging me right now?"*

Her response was quick and genuine, *"No, but I do feel guilty."*

"Maren, what the fuck did you do?"

Then she dropped the ball that she probably should've had a while ago. *"Jack, first, you know how I always had a crush on her. I went over there one day to see the baby and her. The baby was sleeping and as we had some coffee and chatting, I noticed she was stressed. After asking, she is indulging how she was frustrated that not only your work consumes you, but you never are home. Well, I..."*

"Well, what, Maren? Did you do what I think you did with my wife?"

She giggled then. *"Oh god no. I would never do that to you. I merely told her that if she wasn't happy that she should give you an ultimatum. I never thought she would skip over that and just leave you. I'm sorry, Jack."*

"I'm not upset with you, Maren. Can you at least next time give me the heads up, please? What's important is that you keep an eye on that house this week."

She was happy after I wasn't mad. *"I can do that, Jack. You said 71 High Street? I will start today. What do you want me to report to you?"*

"No, it's 72 High Street. Please report anything that's out of the norm. I've got to run. Please call me with anything."

I looked at the time as I was on more edge now and it was eight thirty. I really didn't want to go home yet. I thought if I waited until ten when the next shift came on, I could possibly make it a late night. I looked over the pending paperwork that had been piling up on my desk for a week now and the deeper I got into it, the more I thought that I hadn't seen Marylin's report on the Andrea murder yet. I was just about done when I pulled the last paper; it was her report. Before I got in depth on reading it, I poured myself a shot of whiskey and as I sipped on it, I pulled the report in front of me and read. The deeper I got, the more blah and boring it was getting. Until I came upon a part that I found intriguing.

"When I came back from clearing the area I came across what appeared to be a woman who was awaiting on the docks for something to come in from the bay. When I approached her, she told me to go pound sand. I had firmly asked her what her intentions were. With no response, I walked a bit closer to her with my hand on my gun, ready to draw. She turned to me and screamed again to get the fuck away. This time she was wielding a gun and as that was the case, I retreated

behind my car. I was watching her as the boat was getting closer. Just as I was about to reach for my radio, I heard what appeared to be a bloodied scream. I dropped my radio and looked to find the woman on the ground. I ran over to see if she was still alive and when I did, she had seemed to pass away immediately from a wound to the neck."

There were a few things that were odd to me about this. Why did she not report the strangled part of this? I read more until it was finished, and she never reported clearing the scene as well as searching the area for any suspects. She also didn't finish the report that the body went missing, which was intriguing to me as she was so precise with everything. I sat there and pondered this report as I took another shot. I was contemplating my next move in my quiet office, when the phone damn near knocked my ass out of my chair. "Hello, this is chief Donaldson."

"Jack, it's Maren. I just thought I saw some scuffling going on over there."

"Maren, how sure are you?"

She was already on it and was happy but didn't have much yet. "I saw shadows in the window."

"Maren, I can't just run for that. Give me a call when you hear something as well."

I wanted to believe what she saw was correct, but I couldn't go without more. It killed me to be like that to her, but I knew the guy that Alexis was with would feed off seeing me, especially now knowing I knew who he was and possibly up to. I looked up then and saw the third shift coming in and I took advantage of that by leaving for the night. I went home to my empty, quiet house in the farm area as I pulled in. The house being dark didn't really bother me as much as I was missing Abby and how she never deserved to die like that as I knew she would've been the woman for me. Then thoughts of Andrea came through and that she could've been another for me to fill this empty home with. I held thoughts that she might be still alive as she didn't want to get caught up in the heat of being caught. I shrugged it off and went into the house for the night. I drank some more until I fell unconscious on my reclining chair.

Chapter 12

The next morning had come fast and harsh with the sunlight beaming on my now hungover face as I sat up in my chair. I got up for some coffee and put on the television for a few minutes to catch some news.

"....and that's the forecast. Now back to Mandy for some breaking news. Thanks, Curt, yes there has been a report of a missing woman in the town of Ipswich last night. No further details as the police are still searching for her boyfriend."

I lost all feeling in my arms at that moment as I dropped my full cup of coffee all over the living room floor. *FUCK!* I scurried to change into a new uniform as I headed down to the station and when I got there, I was the focus of everyone's attention as all eyes were on me. I didn't pay any attention to them as I made my way into my office and sat to collect my thoughts of what may possibly be going on. I picked up the radio and before I started to radio out to check in with Marylin, the phone rang.

"This is Chief Donaldson."

"Jack, it's Chief Cole from Ipswich police."

"Hey, Craig, please tell me that this does not involve my wife?"

His voice was firm that he didn't want to chat this over the phone. *"When you get a chance, come over and chat with me this morning, please."*

"I'll be over shortly, Craig. Thank you."

So many thoughts ran through my mind at that moment. I was thinking the worst. I was zoned out when the phone almost knocked me out of my chair again when it rang. *"This is Chief Donaldson."*

"Jack, it's Maren. I wanted to say that the Ipswich police were looking to chat with you."

"Tell me something I didn't know. What else do you have?"

She then provided decent information to me before I went to chat to the chief in Ipswich. *"I know that the doctor's SUV is gone, and the front door was wide open, which led to the call to the police."*

"Thanks, Maren. I'm running over to the Ipswich Police Station now. I'll be in touch."

I hopped into my Bronco and started to drive to Ipswich. I thought of how Alexis and I had gotten to this point and my stomach started to churn. *If only I had paid attention to the warning signs of her not being happy in the marriage, maybe perhaps we wouldn't be here in this moment.* I quickly snapped out of it when a loud truck honked at me to get back on my side. I swerved to do so and straightened myself out, before I thought, *no man, this is total bullshit. She put us in this fucking mess. Fuck, and I still have love for her as well. Why would she be so quick to jump on the first cock and ride out of town?* I was pissed but I reigned myself in as I pulled into the police lot. I was greeted when I walked in the front door.

"Come with me to my office, Jack." I had known Craig ever since middle school, and I knew when something was serious because there was no small talk to be had. "Come in, take a seat. Thank you for taking time out of your busy day."

"Have you any news for me, Craig?"

"Well, Jack, as you know with an ongoing investigation, I can't divulge anything yet."

"What the FUCK! Are you being serious right now?" After a long hesitation of looking away from me I was not going to stand this.

"Jack, I assure you I have all my department out looking for her right now. Can I ask you is there any reason why this would happen?"

"Nah, I mean she walked out on me as you probably already heard. To my knowledge, she then shacked up with the doctor that helped me when I had that tussle a bit ago."

He then started in on the normal police bullshit, "Have you guys been fighting?"

"What kind of question is that?"

Raising his hands to calm me then, "I'm just covering all my bases, Jack. Although I don't suspect you, I wanted to allow my due process to come out."

I did calm a bit to answer his bullshit question. "Well, I can understand that as upsetting as it is. But I can assure you that we did not fight an ounce. She was tired of me being on the force and decided that she had enough."

"Ok, thank you, Jack, for answering that question for me. I know this is a difficult time for you right now, and I will be in touch when we find something."

"Thank you, Craig."

Back in the Bronco, I decided I would drive up to the beach where she loved to go when she wanted some peace and quiet. I found myself about ten minutes later at Little Neck Beach. I got out and made my way over to look at the beauty of the still water, until I spotted something by the edge of the water. I made my way and as I got close to it, my stomach turned. It was once her favorite Red Sox hat that I had gotten her when we first started dating. I picked it up and as I did, something else fell out. It was her glasses, which was weird as she never forgot them, just with the thoughts if she needed them. I held them in my hand as I looked all around at the empty beach. The wind blew out of the northeast from over the cool ocean water. As it whistled in my ear, it sounded as though someone, or something was sneaking up behind me. I turned quickly and saw no one there, but I had goosebumps like someone was watching me right then.

I peered all over the surrounding area as there were a lot of places someone could be hiding. I noticed then the clouds got thicker like there was an impending storm coming through. I still saw nothing around, but I still felt eyes upon me, which was giving me an uneasy feeling, so I made my way back to the Bronco. I turned the key and started it as I sat there looking out at the ocean, lost for what seemed like forever.

BANG! A loud thud against my window had me almost piss my pants with terror. I looked over and it was a seagull that rammed right into my window. I was watching it as it struggled at first, but thankfully, it shook itself off and went flying away. I hated to see animal accidents. I thought how crazy that was and the last time it had happened we were getting ready to have a huge Nor'easter. I then decided it was best to drive back to the station and check in with our team.

When I got back, it was almost a ghost town. Apart from the receptionist and the janitor, there was no one else there to check in on. I went into the lunchroom and turned on the television as it was close to dinner and the news was on talking about the impending weather. *"Now let's get over to what appears to be a busy night ahead for you, Richard."*

"Thank you, Cindy. Yes, indeed we have a classic strong Nor'easter coming in as we speak right now. The rain will be heavy as we are looking at three to four inches of rain accompanied by tropical storm force winds that could make travel difficult and not to mention power outages and coastal flooding."

I had heard enough as I looked around the office to see if Marylin was back. Fuck, I forgot she was still away until tomorrow. I picked up the phone and called to see if she could come back.

She picked up the phone in a sexy voice like she was expecting me, *"Hello."*

"Marylin, it's Jack."

She was missing me as I was her. "Hey stranger, how are you?"

"Well, I've been a bit preoccupied today. I just learned of this huge storm coming in and I could use some sleep before it really hits."

She was hesitant but warmed by hearing me. *"Uh, sure. I can come back by eight. Is that OK?"*

"That's fine, Marylin. Thank you."

I turned around and there was George. George was my go-to information guy, an intel person. He could usually find things at his fingertips that no one usually could. "Hello, George, you just scared the fucking crap out of me. Please don't sneak up on me like that."

Smiling now at me, he said, "Sorry, sir, I wanted to give you the latest on the storm. It will be a good-sized one as you know. It is forecasted to bring high tides that will cause flooding as well as hurricane force winds. What do you think our plan of attack is for the town?"

"This will not be a good one. I'd say check in with the town and make sure if boats need to be pulled that they do it by sundown, before it gets bad. I will also check in with people by the coast."

He was happy to do whatever I asked of him as he smiled at me again. "I can do them both, sir. I mean, if you have anything more on your plate."

"Ok, thank you, George." After he left, I decided to peek at the local news and the radar was showing a huge expansion of thunderstorms just offshore. Shit, I looked at the time and it was only quarter of six, so I decided to go get some food for the station down at Callahan's Clam Shack. I was barely crossing the causeway when I noticed the water was already up in the road. The causeway was known to flood severely during storms like this, but I had not seen it this high this early in a while. I quickly made it to Callahan's and ordered a huge amount of food that would get us through the storm and about a half hour had passed when I finally got to leave. When I got to the middle of the causeway, the water was just starting to splash over. I slowly drove through the flowing water that was washing through our tiny causeway that was one of the two ways to the other side of the town. The other way was a street called Apple Street. Apple Street was known for its winding turns in the middle of nowhere as well as the part near my house that was flood vulnerable. Once in a blue moon, it would surprise flood over there and I had a feeling it might during this one.

Thankfully, I made it through the causeway before the flooding really took over and as I was about to turn towards the station, I stopped and looked out my rearview mirror to see the water completely submerge the road and all the dry surface that was left there as it looked like a flowing river now. The night was going to be long and when I went inside with the food, I saw Aaron and Sully, my part time officers, getting ready to take on what the night may have in store for us. "Hey guys, can you do me a huge favor right now?"

"Sure, what is it boss?"

"Bring two cars on either side of the causeway and block them off please."

They looked surprised as it was still early to do so in their eyes. "You really think we need to do that already?"

"Aaron, yes I just watched the water submerge the whole road within twenty minutes."

They immediately went on alert. "Shit! We got you. We are on it."

"Hey, I will get Marylin to pick you boys up."

They had left and I was about to pick the phone up to call Marylin, when I heard, "Hey, Jack, were you getting ready to give me another call?" She smiled as she gave me a small hug before she sat down at my desk with me.

"Uh, no. That was a crazy question." I grinned at her as she knew me like a book.

She came out with the question she always asked before a storm that would affect the town would hit, "You think this storm will be that bad?" She knew I had a bearing for the weather and its intensity that it can bring around here.

"Yes, I do think it will be worse than what they think. We need to be prepared." Just then, we heard something crash against the roof. "What the fuck was that?"

She peeked out of the window. "That was the tree in the back crashing down in our back parking lot. You should come see the wind already." It was relentless as the winds were constant already and it was only seven.

"You should go pick up Aaron and Sully."

Surprised that they had been out already in the weather, I asked, "What, where did they go?"

"Oh, I knew there was something I wanted to ask. I sent them to put their cruisers down at the causeway to block it off."

"Jack, this early?"

"Marylin, just go get them as you will then see for yourself why." I had to be as serious as can be as they hadn't realized how bad this storm was going to be.

"Ok, I will go. Let me ask you, though, are you ok to ride this storm out here? I ask because you look exhausted."

"I think I should be fine."

"Jack, at least consider going home when I get back with them." She then left as the storm got heavier by the minute.

Sitting got me exhausted as I finished my portion of the dinner I got for the station. So, I got up to take a walk out to the lobby. I saw my crew just coming in and they were ready for a very harrowing night within this storm. Then I heard my radio go off.

"Jack, are you there?"

"Marylin, yes, I'm here. How is it going out there?"

"Well, the good news is that I do have both of our boys and we are heading back."

"Uh, what's the bad news?"

She was scared about how I'd take this next one as you can hear the hesitance in her voice, *"Their cars will be submerged very shortly and there was nothing we could do about that!"*

"Shit! Really?"

"Yeah, I'll explain more when I get back. FUCK! This is not good!"

"What is it?! Are you ok?"

"Jack, we are fine, but I will see you in about ten minutes. We do have to chat though." The radio went silent after that. I hope things weren't as bad out there as I think they are. I guess this will be a very long ten minutes.

Chapter 13

My walk around the office became pacing after ten minutes went by and then fifteen minutes and no sign of them. *"Jack, this is Craig. Are you there?"*

"Craig, what is wrong? I'm here and just waiting for my deputy to come back."

His voice was thankfully calming. *"Nothing is wrong. I wanted to check in to see how you guys are holding up down there?"*

I looked out of the office just then and it was already dark. The window was just pure water from the rain. *"Oh, we are just fine. The usual already with the causeway flooding. Nothing we can't handle."*

He was assuring his calming presence then. *"If you need anything at all, just give us a shout."*

"Thank you, Craig." Another fifteen minutes went by and most of the force was scattered around town when I saw Marylin's car pull in. *Thank God they are back and safe.* They were in their rain slickers and looked like drowned rats when they got in. "Are you all ok?" They nodded with grins on their faces as Aaron and Sully went down to shower and change into fresh clothes. Meanwhile, Marylin followed into my office as

we both sat. "Marylin, what the fuck went on out there?"

"Jack, you won't believe me when I do tell you. But the first issue was when I got to the other side by Callahan's to pick up Sully, there was a person closing the restaurant across the street that hadn't realized they were quickly surrounded by water; the river was angry down there. We safely got her to dry ground, not without all our effort, and that's the reason why those two are heading to change. I will be too after our chat. The other thing was that the lower end of Apple Street was filling with storm water. You should think about hunkering down at home tonight."

"Oh, and miss this fun?"

"Jack, we're more than capable of handling things here tonight. I mean, we do have the chance to call Ipswich if we need some extra people. You look exhausted. How much sleep have you had in the past week? I bet very little! Have you heard anything on Alexis, if she has surfaced yet?"

I wanted to skirt her suggesting me to go home as long as possible, "Oh, I guess that cat is out of the bag now that you know about Alexis missing. No, there's no word on her where abouts yet and not even her boyfriend either."

Just then she came over and put her hands on my shoulder as she whispered in my ear, *"I'm sorry that*

that has added to your trouble. I hope she is found safe and sound. But you need to go get your rest. You can trust me tonight. I promise I will let you know if you're needed. Just go home." Then she sealed it with a juicy kiss to my ear.

I hated to admit that she was right. "You're right, it has been a rough week for me and thank you for those kind words about Alexis. It means a lot." I looked at her as she gave me a stern face that I better listen to her. "Alright, I will go home, but I will have my radio on if you need me AT ALL. Please call me."

"You bet I will." She gave me a smile as I packed up my things and an extra gun and headed out in the monstrous storm for home. I pulled out of the parking lot and slowed down as I couldn't believe what I saw. The marshland behind the station and town hall was submerged now with water billowing in. I stepped on the gas to make my way towards Apple Street as after a few minutes of hauling ass I was slowed down by a tree already collapsed in someone's yard. Normally, it wouldn't be an issue, but it was a large Maple tree that was half in the road. *"Marylin, you do not have to answer me, but I wanted to let you know that you need to get somebody down here near Pickering Street as there is a Maple halfway across the road."*

She was quick to respond, *"Over and out, Jack. Thank you, I will get someone out there as soon as possible. Now get home safe."*

I moved like there was someone chasing me as the rain started to make things become blinding in the wind. I finally made it to Apple Street and the brook was getting to be a flowing river. This was better at least as I had the trees shielding the rain from making it blind, but I had to dodge branches down all over the place in the road as I wound through the wooded long street towards the end. But as I approached what I was nervous about, the marshland, I saw what I couldn't believe. The water was about a foot deep over the road with minor wave action from the wind. I inched my way through as I saw the end of the road which led to Southern Ave and seconds away from my house. The fact that this spot was a few miles inland and the water was this intense was startling.

I pulled into my driveway to find a tree down in the backyard, but everything else was intact for now, thankfully. The house seemed dark and empty as I walked up to the front door in sheets of rain now, I looked over where Alexis used to sit waiting for me to come home at night. I stared for the longest time, wondering if she was found yet and if she was ok until a huge flash of light and a loud crash of thunder snapped me out of my dazed thoughts. I unlocked the door and went inside from the storm.

I turned on the kitchen light and worked my way up the circular stairwell towards the bathroom for a hot shower to try to forget the stress of the week. I was halfway through the shower when I heard the wind whipping up outside with thunder getting louder and I prayed that Marylin was staying safe. I hoped for the same wherever Alexis was with the baby. I was in deep thought enjoying the hot water flow over my head when there was a creaking sound like someone was walking upstairs.

"HELLO, who's there?" No answer and that was kind of stupid of me as I then knew my tiredness had crept up on me. "Stupid idiot, if there is anyone in the house, they are not going to answer me and besides it probably was the storm."

I finished up and got out of the shower. I felt a lot better until I went to grab my spare handgun under the bathroom sink and it wasn't there. I did not panic yet as I usually moved them and more than likely forgot the hiding spot for now. I made my way out of the bathroom and grabbed my pistol that I carried every day and made my way around each room to make sure everything was secure. I searched all the open spaces and rooms until I felt that the house was clean. I wanted to do one more check with Marylin as I grabbed my radio while my soup was heating up. *"Marylin, I wanted to check to see how things are going down there?"*

"Oh, hey, Jack, this is Sully. She is patrolling the town right now and will be back shortly."

"Ok, just let her know if she needs anything at all to not hesitate to reach out."

It was unlike Marylin to go out to patrol, let alone in a storm, and as I ate my soup, I wondered what she was up to. However, I was glad she had Aaron with her. I decided to grab a beer from the refrigerator after cleaning up and made my way to the living room. I sat my ass in much awaited recliner time as the news was on and blaring about the storm. They had people out along the coastline reporting the conditions, and I thought, *Man, Alexis considered my job dangerous and look at these people*. I quickly passed out and didn't know how long I had slept because when I awoke, the power was lost. The only light was from the thunderstorm happening now. The light was just enough to see the outside from where I was sitting as I checked my watch, 11:30. I was wide awake now watching the storm and I went to the kitchen and grabbed another beer. I stood there at my kitchen sink watching the rain stream down throughout my yard, making my driveway a huge mud pile.

I went to grab both of my guns and placed them on the counter next to the sink as it was a reaction with the power being out. As I was in full sip of my beer, I heard a creak in my bedroom. I went to go check it out and it was just the wind finding a way through the window. I breathed a sigh of relief and went back to the kitchen. I stood there by the window as the thunderstorm had subsided for a moment, when suddenly I felt something around my neck and pulling to try to choke me. The struggle was real as I was trying to keep my fingers between the rope and my throat so this person wouldn't be successful. Suddenly, there was a huge rumble of thunder off in the distance and then with an instant a flash of lightning that lit up the whole kitchen. I saw the position of the person's legs behind me and as that flash dimmed, I lunged forward towards the counter as I brought this person down.

The grip was still there but not as tight as I used all my energy to wrestle out of the lock. When I stood up, I reached around for my guns. They weren't there suddenly, and I was a bit thrown off as I only knew of the one person I was just wrestling with. But I hadn't the time to think about it. I found the closest weapon, a baseball bat I kept behind the toaster after Alex had left, and I turned around. As I swung, I was just swinging at air. I looked to see if this person was still there on the floor, but they weren't there, as if they had quietly disappeared. As I reached into my belt to grab my flashlight, I heard a knife scrape metal.

The storm picked up in intensity yet again with more thunder and lightning as I was searching through the rooms by flashlight for the person who just tried to strangle me. I cleared the living room and bedroom and as I made my way back out into the kitchen, I heard a creak in the stairwell off the kitchen that led to the basement. Just as I got close to the door, a huge flash of lightning that struck a tree nearby forced me to be a bit jumpy for a second and as I gained control of myself, I reached for the door to the basement. A hand reached out to grab me. I turned and as I did, I shoved off on this person enough that I flashed the light towards them. The darkness was great that I couldn't get a clear glimpse of them at first as they almost eluded the flashlight to their advantage.

I peered at this person from the darkness of the kitchen and what I saw was a dark-hooded person standing there looking back at me. I couldn't believe the serial killer was here in my kitchen attempting to kill me. But why? We both stood there in the dark staring at each other, awaiting the first move made. We inched ever so slightly forward towards each other as I was still wielding my bat and the hooded killer was carrying a knife. I got a foot away from the killer and noticed this person was a bit shorter than me as the lightning was fiercely lighting the place like a photo shoot, wearing black sweatpants to match the hoodie. They were getting antsy with how close we were when I heard a door open behind me. Someone came lunging out as they tried tackling me then mistakenly tackled the other hooded person. They were both moaning and startled as they were both wearing black hooded sweatshirts. I now heard a women's voice as they both stood.

There was only one person that sounded like that. "Alexis?!" As they both stood up, the power started to flick on and off. She stood there for a second and undid her hood. She was now standing there in front me holding the knife in hand and giving me a death stare. "What in the fuck is going on?" I reached for the other person's hood and revealed it was her boyfriend. "Are you guys for real? I was worried sick; I mean and now what I'm seeing…"

"You really are so fucking dumb, aren't you? Sit the fuck down and take what we will do to you like a man!"

I hadn't listened to her as I knew if I had sat, I would be toast. "Alexis, why would you be here trying to kill me, let alone doing this to innocent people? Have you been the person doing this to people?"

The doctor pushed me down into the kitchen chair when the lights came back on and now Alexis was staring at me with a grin on her face. "All of those nights I was by myself; do you really think I was sitting here on the front porch waiting for your stupid ass? No, I was out cleaning up the world, doing your dirty work that you were not doing." I shot her a pissed off look as I was about to say something when her boyfriend punched me in the face and I bit my tongue, "Oh and it was my fucking pleasure to have killed the two women you were falling for after I dumped your ass. You don't deserve to be in a relationship with anyone! I really think if you gave me that attention that you gave them our sex life would be existent but no you had to be married to your fucking job. So, with that I went out there cleaning up this fucking town and around the area so maybe once you'd come home to me! You ask why I'm with a drug dealer? Well, the answer is he is a better lover in life than you will ever be to me! He supports me killing these awful people who ruined my life!"

The doctor knew I was going to get loud as he then started to punch me senselessly when he stopped.

Alexis was behind me when the doctor said something that I would never forget. "Your wife has been my love for a very long time, and I thank you for not being around so I can get to know her. She had my child, and we will get married as soon as she does what she needs to do with you! Once she's done with you the serial killing will be done!"

All that I could get out now amid my bloodied face was, "You piece of shit!"

She started to whisper in my ear as she held the knife up to the side of my neck, *"You will soon be resting in hell, you piece of shit. Did you really think I was in love with you? If you must know why I did all of this, well let's see, Andrea and her crew, they are all Fred's competition. You see, you were about to fuck all my magic up. I never loved you, Jack; I just used you to get what we wanted and the people I killed deserved what they got! Now you will get what's coming to you! Don't worry, I have the baby safely with his parents, well Fred, and my baby. I know and you're wondering about why Abby, well that fucking slut had it coming, that's all I have to say!"*

I was shocked at what I was hearing and speechless. I saw someone pull into the driveway; I wanted to stall Alexis from ending my life now. "It doesn't have to be this way!"

"Shut the fuck up and take this like a man!" She raised the knife ever so slightly when suddenly a loud

boom came from the porch as the window shattered and Alexis dropped to the floor.

"NOOOO!!!!" The doctor went lunging at the porch, carrying a gun, but then another shot came from the porch, and he dropped in his tracks.

"JACK!!!!" I was slumped in the chair as I was gathering myself when Marylin was yelling my name from the front porch and soon before I could snap out of it, she was standing in front of me. "Jack, are you ok?"

I took a minute to speak as she gazed into my eyes and instantly melted my heart. "Yes, I'm fine. Thank you for the save." She helped me stand and as I looked around at the broken glass mess as well as the bloodied bodies on my kitchen floor, with one of them being Alexis, I was in shock still at what had just gone down. "How did you, oh my god I have so many questions for you when I can think clearly." I looked at the doctor as he had a pool of blood surrounding him now from a single shot to his chest. This should've been a restful night. Then I was about to peer over to Alexis when she was sitting upright now with blood dripping from her hand and her upper chest as she was struggling from a shot to her shoulder.

She gave all her strength to talk as she was getting weaker by the moment. "You are a fucking asshole. What in the hell did you do to me?"

I looked at her with anger then, "Alexis, I have, or should I say, we have so many questions for you."

"Fuck you!" Suddenly, she grabbed a gun from her waistline and as she was about to point, there was a loud bang from behind me. Alexis's lifeless body smashed once again on what was our kitchen floor. I looked over her, blood pooling around her lifeless body from a direct wound to the head, and thought about all the good times we had as I just wanted to ask were they fake? I watched as her brains were splattered all over the kitchen cabinets as her beautiful hair was now red with brain fragments through them. Suddenly, I felt a hand on my shoulder.

"Jack, I'm so sorry. She gave me no choice."

"It's fine, Marylin. I knew it was her or I."

We stood there looking at the scene while we gathered ourselves. "Jack, can I ask where your baby is?"

"I'm not totally sure where the baby is, Marylin. She claimed it was with his parents. They also claimed that the baby wasn't even mine as it was the doctors. But how much of that can I believe from a drug dealer and a serial killer. We should call this one in as you know it will take a bit for people to get here and when you do, please put out the information that there is a child somewhere out there to search for when the storm starts to subside." When the coroner's office arrived, the feds and all other police agencies processed the scene and took our statements about what happened. It was finally five in the morning when the last of the people left. I turned to Marylin as she was sitting patiently in the kitchen chair, she pulled me up from. "You can leave. I'm sure you have had enough of this shit for one night."

"Jack, I will leave after you get some sleep for a few hours. I know that a lot has happened here to make it difficult to get to sleep but with the way the tide is right now it would make sense for you to stay and rest here. Besides, I have Craig down at the station right now making sure things are being run."

I knew enough not to fight with her as I did need some shut eye before I dealt with everything that would be on my plate after this. "Ok but wake me by seven so we can ride in together, please."

She gave me a warm smile. "Absolutely, I wouldn't have it any other way. I can and will hang here so you can do that."

Chapter 14

I had the best sleep of my life as I dreamt of Alexis and myself together. We were kissing passionately when I opened my eyes. Marylin was kneeling by my bed with her lips and tongue locked with mine until she noticed I was awake. She pulled slowly away from me as I was still staring and wondering what and where this came from. She started to pull back as she saw my facial expression. "I'm sorry, I couldn't resist."

I smiled at her to reassure her that it was ok. "No, that was, that was perfectly fine. You just caught me by surprise. What time is it?"

She breathed a sigh of relief. "It is seven thirty, I gave you an extra half hour. I hope you don't mind I was watching you sleep. How are you?"

"Well, I do feel better now with some rest after that. What time did everyone leave?"

"Oh, they just finished up about an hour ago." She yawned a bit after but was bright-eyed even after the longest night each of us had.

"Marylin, we should try to get to the station to deal with all the crap that's on our plate today."

She looked glad to hear me wanting to get back at it as she made me feel better just then. "That sounds fine. I do believe I heard Apple Street is back open now, so we don't have to go Route 128."

We hopped in our respective vehicles and as she followed me down the start of Apple Street, I couldn't help coming to a stop as I looked where the water had submerged the road. I couldn't believe it as mud and branches as well as a few boulders were scattered on the side of the road. *"Everything ok up there, Jack?"*

"Ah, yes, it is. I was just admiring with surprise how bad the street got in last night's storm. Are you sure we had enough coverage?"

"Yes, why? Can we please proceed to get this day started!"

"Uh, sorry, I just didn't want to walk into a blindsided shit storm because we had residents without an officer."

"JACK, like I said, we had Ipswich and Hamilton assisting us last night. Can we just go?"

I hadn't pushed it as we proceeded through the winding street, avoiding tree branches down throughout the street until we made it safe to the other side. We took the quick right onto the main street and what seemed like a lifetime was only a five-minute drive until we reached the station. When we pulled in, there were state police there as well as the feds and they were all awaiting our arrival. It had made me feel better seeing the coverage that was there; although, I wasn't expecting what was coming. I walked in and headed towards my office. As I put my hat on the desk, Craig came in and sat. "Jack, I'm terribly sorry about how things ended up for you. If there's anything I can do for you, please let me know."

Craig sat there for a few minutes awaiting me to say something, but I hadn't known what to say so I came out with the only thing I could, "Thank you, I will call you in a few days." He got up and left. I had some peace for an hour and enjoyed a strong cup of coffee when I noticed an FBI agent finishing up with Marylin. He knocked and came in to see me.

"Jack, Agent Carr again, how are you doing?"

"Pleasure to see you again, Agent Carr. Please have a seat."

He got right to the point as I was sure he wanted to get going after that crazy night, "Oh, thank you. This will not take long, I promise. Two things, can you tell me if you had any knowledge of your wife and her boyfriend being serial killers? Can you also tell me if you might have known of his Cartel status?"

"Why would you ask that? Wait, I understand. To answer your ridiculous question, NO I had no idea that they were serial killers. The answer to your other question as ridiculous as it is no, I hadn't known his Cartel involvement." What more could I say, I didn't indulge to him I knew of him dealing drugs. I mean that was my business here in town and they didn't care that much for our quaint town.

He was polite after what could've been me yelling. "Well thank you for that. My next question is, do you feel you are ok right now being chief?"

"Yes, why would you ask this?"

He smirked politely in his answer then. "Jack, I apologize if I upset you, but you have been through a lot recently and if you weren't up to it, we could post here for a while until—"

I then interrupted him before he could finish, "I'm fine. I appreciate you asking, but I'm fine. Is there anything else?"

He took a deep breath and said something I wasn't expecting, "Yes, since your department was the ones who ended this, I was wondering if you would head the announcement on TV?"

"Sure, that would be wonderful." I had more energy than I should have at that moment with the feeling that I could deliver this news not only to our town but the state of Massachusetts.

"Great because they will be here in about a half hour."

"Before you go, can you help me with one thing, Agent Carr?"

Happy to oblige, he answered, "What is it?"

"I need help locating my child that my wife and I had together. She didn't give where abouts before she was killed."

He was startled by this news. "Oh my god! Are you serious! Why didn't anyone put this in the details?"

"Because I wanted it under wraps for security as this has been a shit storm running amuck here in town too long for people to be frantic again."

"I assure you I will put my best people out there on this and keep this between us. I also assure you that there's no more leak in our department." I believed him, which was a far cry when I had the first feds in my office months ago.

He left and with what he said assured me enough to get a bit more comfortable before the reporters came and Marylin had noticed as she came buzzing in and sat down abruptly. "Marylin, can you give me a report on what town looks like?"

"You don't need to worry about that right now."

"MARYLIN! PLEASE LET ME KNOW! IF I HAVE TO DRIVE AROUND IT WILL NOT BE GOOD!"

She then reported to me reluctantly as she didn't want this on my plate right now, "Well, the causeway took some damage in the storm as there is a piece of it that got washed out. The other is that half the town is without power right now. Before you ask if there's anything being done, we have had power crews out since early this morning restoring power and as far as the causeway, we have a crew working on it right now. They are hopeful to have it back up in a few days."

"Thank you, was that so hard. Oh fuck!"

"What is it?"

"I think we're up on giving a briefing! Let's go." We went outside the front of the building as there was a podium there with Agent Carr and a state police officer next to him. "Hello folks, as you know we have an update on the serial killer but before we give it over to Chief Donaldson, we want to remind you it has been a long rough twelve hours all our departments have had. So, I ask you to not press the questions if we say we can't respond to them yet. Now, without further ado, I welcome the Chief."

"Hello, ladies and gentlemen of the press. Thank you all for being here. As you know, we have had a run in with the serial killers. Last night, they attempted to take an officer's life, but before it happened, they were shot and killed instantly." All was quiet within the crowd until I was about to say the last of my sentence; one guy spoke from the back.

"Can you tell us if that officer was you, Chief?"

I stood there and tried to see who it was but couldn't see where it came from, so I avoided the question as we had to wrap up the investigation. "So, it was difficult as you all know with the storm going on last night and power that was lost and roads flooded out, we couldn't get the word out until now that the town, and the region, is safer now without these monsters stalking innocent people again. I ask you all to be patient as we work to finish the investigation as well as clean our town again to get you the final answers." That was my first news briefing ever in my life and never thought it would ever happen, but it was done as I walked back into the station to all the reporters trying to fire questions at me, but I ignored them all as Agent Carr told them that was it. I sat down in my office while Marylin made sure all that attended had left, then she came in to sit with me.

She gave her genuine sexy caring glance to me. "How are you doing?"

"I'm ok, why?"

She didn't take too long after things subsided to ask me her all-important question, "Just checking in as I care. Why don't you come over for dinner tonight?"

I sat there and stared into her beautiful blue eyes. I hated myself for doubting that she was not the person who I thought she was. "Yes, that would be fine."

"Good, I hope you are in the mood for burgers and beer."

My stomach was then turned on by that thought. "Yes, that sounds good."

"I'll see you around six then!" She tried to slip in the fact that she wouldn't be there the rest of the day.

"Yes, why are you leaving?"

"Yes, you see it is my day off as you told me to take it off after the night we had. Well, that's what you said while sleeping." She left and she had a smirk on her face as if she was about to have me over a barrel or something. I found myself watching her ass as she walked out to her car and left, then there was a knock at my door.

"I'm sorry to bother you, Chief, but I have a phone call for you."

After they shut the door, I quickly answered, *"This is Chief Donaldson. How can I help you?"*

"Chief, I hope you get some rest because my people will run that town soon enough!" The line went dead after that, and I wondered who that was; they clearly had their voices muffled. *Is there more trouble coming and when will it be?* I remembered Andrea's guy Frank saying he would be back next year but what about Andrea as we never found her body. Either way, I would have some time to be ready for it.

The day got away from me as I had more law enforcement coming in and out and calling to ask if I needed anything. It felt great at first, but after a while, I just wanted not to answer any of them as they took up most of the day. Soon it was quarter to six already. I was a bit excited to get the hell out of the station for once, get some good food, and relax with Marylin.

Before I made my way, I took the plunge after all that went down at home to go and get changed. As I made my way into the driveway, it all seemed empty. I looked around at the house and then the front porch where Alexis greeted me day after day. I also reminisced about the time I had rushed Alexis to the hospital when she was giving birth. I sat there in a daze until a wind gust blew a huge branch down in front of me. I looked up at the big circular tree in the middle of the yard to see it was weakened by the storm. *"Well, put that on my to do soon list,* I thought and went inside the house. When I stepped up on the front porch, it was surreal seeing the broken window that was now boarded up. "How could you do this to us, Alexis?" I shrugged off the thoughts as I realized I was talking to myself and went inside. I looked in the kitchen at all that was torn apart; I saw the two body outlines from the crime scene that was cleared. I got chills up my spine and then the phone rang.

"Hello?"

Marylin was calling and checking in on me. *"Jack, are you still coming over?"*

"Yes, I stopped home to get changed first. I'll be there shortly." I didn't give her time to ask if I was ok as I just hung up and went to get changed. I was just about done when I finally stared at our bed and envisioned the nights I had with Alexis, whether it was chatting or nights of passion. I missed her in a way, not that I wanted her back, but I just missed her face and touch and was angered as well with the outcome as this was a change that I'll need time to get used to. I finished and made my way out to the Bronco and as I pulled away, I knew what I needed to do with the house, but I knew I needed a bit more time.

I found myself in no time in Marylin's driveway as she was already at the front door with a huge smile on her face. "Hello, it's about time you found your way. How are you doing?"

"Fine, why?"

"Oh nothing, just making small talk." She gave me a hug and a nice warm kiss on the cheek as we both went in. She had dinner already set up for us as there were burgers in the middle of the table with rice and salad.

"This looks amazing. Thank you." We sat and fixed our burgers, then when I started to eat, she spoke.

"I'm sorry about the kiss this morning. I was feeling the need to let you know I was there in more ways than one. I know that wasn't the right time for that."

Awkwardly, I grinned as I gathered my thoughts as I didn't want to say anything stupid. "It's fine, Marylin. It felt good but you caught me by surprise like you had said with the night that was just had. However, for now I think we should keep our relationship strictly professional."

"That's fine, but you better consider me as a friend outside of work." She was hoping for a casual thing, and she didn't have to say those words.

"Sure, that's fine. We can have that casual thing. Can I ask you though, not to change the subject, have you had any sense that Andrea's men might be coming back into town? Also have we had any sense that Andrea had popped up again?"

She looked at me, squinting her eyes as if she was thinking. "No, but I'll keep my eyes open. How are you doing after all that went on? Do you still think that she faked her death?"

"I'm fine! Can you not ask me anymore how I'm doing? To answer your question about Andrea, yes, I believe she somehow faked her death and is still out there. I believe eventually we will see and hear from her again. Awkward silence proceeded after I said that, until I broke the silence when dinner was done. "I wanted to at least say thank you for being there to save my ass though. Can I ask how you knew to be there?"

She smiled and gave me a wink before she responded, "You're very welcome. I guess the only hunch I had was correct and perhaps I should start going with them like you always taught me to."

"But there was no indication that was going to happen. I'm so impressed and thankful."

She was subtle with her answer as she was blushing then, "Enough about that, Jack. I want to say that I think you should take some time off to gather yourself."

The moment she said that I knew why she had me over. "You trying to tell me something?"

She then smiled nervously. "Yes, it was brought to my attention after something of this caliber that happens, we need to give some time off."

I was looking at her in sadness that I would be away and had not thought it was to help. "Fuck, seriously? My fake wife who was a secret serial killer that almost kills me dies and now, I'm being told to take some time off! How much time are we looking at?"

She was firm but felt bad as it was written across her face. "They will reassess you in February!"

I dropped my napkin on the table as my appetite was lost after this. As I looked at her, it was as if she knew what my next move would be. I was almost to the door before she put her arms around my chest from behind. "Jack, I promise I will keep you filled in on everything." I turned around as I was face to face with her then. She smelled super delicious as the scent was a vanilla rose of some sort. She then leaned into me and laid her lips on mine as we stood there for what seemed like an eternity, lip locked, until I slowly moved back.

"Thank you for dinner. I will clean my office and it's all yours until I can come back. I will be in touch."

I then left to clean up my office. As I looked at it before I shut the light and the door, the station was eerily empty of people. I made my way out, started the Bronco, and drove home. When I arrived, I smiled and made my way in for what would seem like a very long winter ahead. I sat for hours looking out over the moonlit fields in my backyard until I fell asleep that night, normally for once and knowing things would be ok in time.

Made in the USA
Middletown, DE
22 March 2024